MYSELF, FOUR TIMES

THE GERMAN LIST

MARIA LAZAR

Myself, Four Times

TRANSLATED BY
ISABEL FARGO COLE

Seagull
BOOKS
LONDON NEW YORK CALCUTTA

Seagull Books, 2026

First published posthumously in German as
Viermal Ich by Maria Lazar

Orignal German edited and compiled by Albert C. Eibl

First published in English translation by Seagull Books, 2026

ISBN 978 1 8030 9673 5

British Library Cataloguing-in-Publication Data
A catalogue record for this book is available from the British Library.

Typeset by Seagull Books, Calcutta, India

CONTENTS

NOTE FROM THE EDITOR

This English translation is based on the first German edition, published posthumously by the Vienna-based publishing house Das vergessene Buch in 2023 under the title *Viermal ICH*. The original typescript was found among Maria Lazar's posthumous papers, which until the end of 2022 were kept at the home of her granddaughter Kathleen Dunmore in Nottingham lag and are now held by the Austrian Exile Library at the Vienna Literature House. Only one carbon copy exists.

The author does not use quotation marks for direct speech, instead marking dialogue with dashes. This idiosyncrasy has been retained, as the blurring of boundaries between actual speech and the narrator's stream of consciousness adds to the special, poetic dynamics of Lazar's prose.

Albert C. Eibl

Translated by Isabel Fargo Cole

Myself, Four Times

The first time it happened was when I was small. Twelve. We had a kitchen maid called Julie. Julie Horky. But the cook's name was Julie too, so Horky's what we called her. Just plain Horky.

It was summer and hazy and dusty and we were heading off to the countryside. To some big hotel, high in the mountains where it was sure to rain. Horky stood there in the front hall, ready to say goodbye, wearing a fresh, paper-stiff white blouse. Her skin gleamed like she'd just rubbed it with liquid candlewax, and her strawy hair was pulled back tight. Horky was good, foursquare and solid as a crate. And now she stood there, expecting me to give her a kiss.

Because every day on my way to school I'd give her a kiss in the front hall and she'd hand me the bread and butter for my snack. That kiss would taste of soft soap and coarse flour. I actually liked to kiss her, I think.

But today two huge leather suitcases were standing between me and her and Mama was giving orders and Papa had his wallet out and my sister Bea was waving from the car at the gate. Worst of all, Uncle Max was gazing down at me, dark and terribly tall, with that certain special smile playing about his lips, and so I couldn't kiss Horky, even though we'd be gone for two months, I just couldn't, I bounded past her out onto the street.

The last I saw as we turned the corner, she was standing outside the house, waving. Her arm was round and unshapely, like a thick branch. I knew her pallid eyes were swimming red with tears. I knew it without seeing it.

That was the first time it happened.

It was a tepid summer day, the sky drooped down in smothered clouds and our train ran along between colourless fields. My sister Bea was eating a slice of bread with yellow cheese. I fingered the plush of the seats with a strange lump in my stomach, a fist clenching. Horky—oh, now Horky would be sad, awfully sad, because I'd betrayed her. She was looking down at her paper-stiff blouse and I was looking down at breasts that suddenly swelled heavy, smelling the dishwater, feeling the coarse, patched blouse—a cat crouched on the tiled stove's bench, an old woman moaned in a farmhouse bed, men's rough voices, endless rain over yellow grainfields, an enormous cow, and my breasts dragged me down, deeper and deeper into humid darkness until the train stopped with a ghastly jolt.

A savage red slash, dripping blood, and I rose to my feet, astonished to be so skinny. Next to Bea's blonde head the compartment's little mirror drew my gaze, someone yelled into the window:—Beer please! I saw a stranger's pale face with deep-set eyes, brows meeting in the middle, childish cheeks and a shockingly old mouth. I turned around. No, there was no one standing behind me. Suddenly I stuck my tongue out. The strange girl, the one in the mirror, stuck her tongue out too. And at that very moment Julie Horky was packing her coarse, flour- and soap-smelling blouses in a wooden suitcase to go back to her Czech village.

While I was travelling with Mama and Papa and Bea to a hotel in the high mountains where it was sure to rain. Why? What for? Why not to a scaldingly blue southern sea? Or a village with a red steeple?

That was the first time.

That evening in the dining room mirror I spied my meagre schoolgirl figure in a colourful crowd of people. Mama said:—Sit up straight. And only much, much later did I learn that Horky must then have been about three months into a pregnancy.

Naturally I'd no idea what had happened, I didn't even guess. All summer long I played with Russian and French children, in secret I read a novel with a lot about love in it that Bea otherwise kept stashed deep in her purse. Horky never crossed my mind any more—I'm not good and noble, certainly not, but I'm not bad either—

I'm nothing, really. And that's just it. That's why I'm writing these notes, or maybe they'll turn into a book, a confession, God knows what. Not that that makes any difference.

The fact is that I'm the one writing here, I am, aren't I, I myself, there's no doubt about it, and whenever I read this, and I'll read it often, perhaps even every evening, like a prayerbook, like a Bible—why the devil should you only read about other people? Horky can write down her own life if she likes, but she'd never dream of it, sitting at home in her factory town, soot and red brick barracks, with six kids or seven, ragged cuticles, the oldest child with water on the brain, and her with a grey blouse, yellowed hair, boozy breath—

But for heaven's sake, what's Horky to me!

I have to pull myself together, have to write about me, me and me alone. A sort of life story. It won't be very interesting, mind. Not that it has to be. Not colourful at all. If only I could write about Grete, that'd be so soft, so sweet, so bright. Swaying evenings under shaded lamps. Or Anette. Gosh, that would be fun, sharp and spiky with a bit of a sting and not always very appetizing, all mixed up with scraps of money. Not to mention Ulla, who's like a crag of salt, crystal clear and cuttingly smart. But what's all this about? This isn't what I want. I want to write about me. Me and me alone.

Because something's got to happen. Especially after yesterday. That was a crime, a sin. But was I the one to blame? Coming home, wasn't it the other girl I saw in the mirror, the stranger I despise? And lying in his arms, was I—no, hush, don't think about it!

But something has got to happen. Because if there's ever a point where I don't just think and feel like the others, I act like them too—that'll be dreadful, that'll be dangerous.

When mirrors fail, shop windows and the glass balls, cut-glass inkwells and polished tabletops, maybe then words will help, the written word. As the saying goes: AND THE WORD BECAME FLESH . . . . . .

Every pencil I write with must serve as a weapon. A weapon against Grete, against Ulla, against Anette, and last but not least against the stranger. And the person writing here is me. Yes, me! Me and me alone!

It seems best to start with my life story, as they call it. Though there isn't any story, really. But that doesn't matter.

The main thing is Uncle Max. It's beside the point how spick and span my nursery was. Every Christmas there were dolls and for every birthday that certain special cake. Mama and Papa got their regular goodnight kiss. It amazes me, really, their being my mother and father. Anyhow, I never called them that. They were simply there like the fire in the stove and the soup on the table.

With Uncle Max it was a completely different matter. He'd suddenly show up, and suddenly he'd vanish. You never knew how long he'd stay, three days, a week, six months or half an hour. Sometimes he'd vanish for an endlessly long time. But the house was always aflutter with excitement: is he coming, will he come this evening or tomorrow or the next day or never come again. Everything having to do with him was so uncertain, so unreliable, so utterly not to be taken for granted.

Of course it makes no sense to claim I know, but I know for sure that when I was still a tiny staring baby he leaned over my crib one time. Late at night. And then he said something, maybe nothing special, but certainly not what one would expect. He probably thought I was pretty ugly, too.

He collected wonderful old Dutch masters, had supposedly painted himself at one time. He didn't like to talk about it and, anyway, it was before I was born.

But apparently when Bea was already quite a big girl, he painted her with a pink gauze ruffle around her neck. Though I never got to see the portrait.

Bea was very pretty, the real daughter of the house, as people put it. Her room was next to mine. She had a jewellery box and a teeny curved-legged writing desk, and letters and photographs always tucked among the lace panties in her dresser. I knew, though I never got a look. She always carried the key around with her. I also knew a man in uniform was involved, a man with broad cheekbones and a pouty lower lip. I know exactly what he looked like. The type who beats his children when his commanding officer gives him a hard time. But I never saw the photo. Really I didn't. Maybe one of the nannies told me about it. Oh, and on the right side he had three gold teeth.

With the nannies it was a bit like with Uncle Max, though they weren't as big and beautiful and fearsome. In my life they lacked the matter-of-fact dependability of Papa and Mama and the grandfather clock in the dining room, the cross-shaped window mullions and Bea. You never knew, one day you might hear:—That creature's got to go! And then the nanny would pack her things and soon she'd be gone, truly gone, forever. Sometimes I even forgot their names.

But I stayed. With my crib, my toothbrush, my little table. I don't know why, but looking back, it's as if I'd slept away my first years open-eyed. Waking up only now and then, with that jolt that makes the ground vanish from under your feet, makes your weightless body drift apart into nothingness. I felt as though I'd been forgotten, in a random house, a random street, with random parents. Often I'd cry over a slice of bread and butter.

Then came the first day of school.

All I knew about school beforehand was that you have to get up early and spend every day with children. So far I'd hardly known any children at all. Everyone tended to forget me, really. Mama had to think about Bea all the time, and Papa had to think about poker and his bank. So school was the first time I was going to be with children. That was exciting. Dangerous. Filled with adventure.

The night before the first day of school I remember we had cold roast rabbit for dinner, with some kind of dark-red sauce. And at 8.55, five minutes before my bedtime, Uncle Max suddenly arrived. He sat next to Bea on the chair that always stood in wait for him, and looked sadly at me with his long slanting eyes when he heard I'd be going to school from now on.—Well, he said, just don't take it too hard.

That frightened me.

Next morning the sun shone cold and glaring and the market women were selling asters. Papa took me to school himself because it was on his way to the bank. My new satchel smelled of hard leather and a tall spinster with bloodless lips received me.

The children—I didn't even see them. All I knew was that a chalkboard loomed in front of me, menacing and black, and names were being written on it. But I knew it as though from a long way away, because sitting beside me on the shiny polished bench—yes, there was Grete.

Grete was so pink, so bright, with such blonde curly hair, like nothing so much as a doll, or a cherub on a greeting card. She smiled with broad white teeth. She was always smiling when she looked at you, really. But she didn't look at me often.

She sat in a cloud of warm haze, a haze of milk and almond soap. I probed that cloud with my skinny brown fingers, but I didn't dare touch Grete herself.

The window beside her cut out a piece of cold bright blue sky. It suddenly struck me that our home had many overly dark curtains. And when the teacher called my name, I didn't hear. She repeated my name. Was that really my name? Grete, Grete, Grete . . . .

All the children laughed, and Grete poked me with her little stroked-smooth fist. The nudge jolted me like an electric shock.

It happened quite often that I'd forget my name. And later, much later, when we were big enough to write numbers on the chalkboard ourselves, I stood up once when the teacher called on Grete and in front of the whole class I solved a math problem in her stead. The children giggled, the teacher stared at me in surprise, but I spoke loud and clear in a gentle, slightly hoarse voice, thinking of a mother in a white dress, with shining eyes. Strange, though, all I saw of that mother was the head and chest, a kind broad bosom, the feet were missing something, the legs weren't there—

Here the teacher interrupted and sent me to my desk. Grete looked at me angrily, not smiling. She had long brown eyes with a reddish light around the pupils.

I didn't meet Grete's mother for real until later. Both her legs were paralysed, she sat smiling in her armchair, directing the whole household, and when she said Grete, her voice sang. And she sewed Grete's shifts herself, stitching decorative hems with endless pains, humming softly, while Grete and her father went on trips or to the theatre. He was a famous professor. Of astronomy. Bright light washed behind shielding milk glass, warming the dining room. The windows' sheer curtains always looked freshly ironed.

As for me, I loved Grete, but there wasn't a thing I could do for her except sneak in tender reddish erasers in my satchel (Radifix, they were called). She liked to nibble them with her broad translucent teeth.

And so, something important had come into my life now that I was going to school. Something almost as important as Uncle Max and almost equally improbable. Only that it was always there, starting at 8 every morning, except when Grete had a sore throat or the sniffles. Anyhow, the first few years Grete and I went to school together, Uncle Max hardly ever showed up any more. At one point he even spent months and months in Egypt. He sent me a postcard with a funny Sphinx on it. I went around with that postcard tied over my heart or rather my stomach with an elastic band until it was all crumpled and illegible.

Once, just before the summer break—the same break that began with the Horky incident—my parents let me hold a big birthday party. To simplify things, I invited two entire rows, because that included Grete as well as Ulla and Anette. I'll have lots to tell about them later. I was all aflutter, because Grete had cancelled several times when she was supposed to come visit, and I couldn't even imagine her light, matter-of-fact beauty in our dark velvet rooms.

It was a mild June afternoon. A whole week's oppressive heat had dissolved into a gentle rain following a brief morning thunderstorm, the black locusts dripped in the park, and my birthday centrepiece was an enormous bunch of snowball blossoms. Snowballs are stupid flowers; when you touch them, they fall off. But you can't buy locust blossoms anywhere.

Grete didn't come until awfully late. She was the very last guest, or almost the last. She wore a white fluffy dress and white shoes despite the rain. Her skin was more delicate than the locust petals and a fine blue vein twitched at her temple. The chocolate bar she brought me was wrapped in glossy blue paper.

Exhausted from the long wait, I huddled in an armchair bathed in cold sweat while she amused herself with the others. They were playing a game in a big circle. Then the doorbell rang again.

Who could that be? Another child? I turned my head to the door and in came—Uncle Max.

He walked up to Grete—first he probably greeted everyone—but he walked up to Grete and stroked her bright hair that fell far down her nape in a streak of delicate gold. He said to someone—What a lovely girl, and in the next circle game he took her hand and played along.

I was still huddled in my armchair, a mirror hanging in front of me, I stared at it, something hurt, a rending pain, and in the mirror I saw Grete float by, holding his hand, floating by all light and bright, high up past the dark cross of the window bars, but Uncle Max's hand was hairy, smelling of hide, brown horses and humid stables. I hated Uncle Max, I was about to rise, tear Grete away from him, do something, something fearsome, sensational—but the circle dissolved, the children wanted to play blind man's buff, they came looking for me and bandaged my eyes.

I daresay there was never such a rainy summer as the one that followed the upsetting birthday party and the farewell scene with Horky. In a big hotel in the mountains, I played with Russian and French children in the library and the hall. We kept darting between the grownups' legs, running away with the magazines and having spats with waiters and liftboys. One morning I woke up late and turned over and Bea's bed was soaked in blood.

I hardly dared to breathe. Outside the window, the clouds hung like dirty scraps of linen. Well, I'd heard about it at school. But all the same—it was ghastly.

Then Bea came in. She turned up the lamp on the nightstand so that the light sliced into my eyes, said:—Shouldn't you be getting up now? and tossed a postcard onto my bed. A card with a hot drunken sky, blinding palaces and a ship. Grete wrote:—How are you? I am well.

Afterwards I took Bea's yellow sunburn powder that was stashed unused in her suitcase and sprinkled a bit on my hand. It was sand, yellow, heat-fragrant sand.

Warm far-away delight trickled all over me.

But that autumn the first day of school brought a huge disappointment. Amid that disappointment, 'it' happened for the second time, and then would happen yet again, over and over—just yesterday—but no, more about that later. It's me who's writing this book, me or the stranger in the mirror, who's always acting so surprised, yes, acting, because in fact she knows everything, knows that just yesterday we were standing together under the cloying blue flowered lamp and I gave him that broad smi . . . —oh goodness, where've I got off to again? I've simply got to, how do you put it, discipline myself. A beastly word, incidentally. I guess I've never had much self-discipline.

So, I was going to tell about that day at school, when after all those years Grete stopped sitting next to me. We'd never been particular friends all that time, but she'd always sat there, always copied my notes, told me about her father and smiled at me with broad teeth. I don't know, to this day I don't know if she was ever fond of me. But I saw and heard her and she seemed to feel that that was enough. Aside from that we'd walk to school together.

But today, on the first day of school, cold with winter fog and the new pencils smelling of hard wood, today she was suddenly sitting in front of me, so straight that the delicate gold down of her nape was right before my eyes, and next to her, impudent and shaggy-headed, slouched Anette, Anette with the ever-moist lips and the Chinese eyes. And not only was Anette sitting beside her, she kept poking Grete with her elbow and giggling. I struggled to choke back my tears. Also, Uncle Max hadn't come the evening before, though he'd phoned to say he would. And next to me sat Ulla, the smartest and ugliest girl, the best athlete in the class.

Why had Grete done this to me? Did she even know what she was doing? I raised my head, and a big soft hand—was it Uncle Max's?—slipped gently, almost tenderly under my chair, lifted me and thrust me into the row in front. My head was tilted to the side and I was smiling, yes, smiling with broad teeth. Red light sparkled in my eyes, my brows lengthened, I was thinking of a blindingly bright evening with a thousand chandeliers, orchestral voices, warm perfume. I sensed something huddling behind me, something dull, aching, bloodily torn, but I wrapped myself in the tepid steam of a bathroom with a milk-glass lamp and heard Anette whisper:—I'd love to go to the opera some day too.

A rattling gunfire volley, I took a bullet in the ribs—the children were laughing and Ulla had nudged me. Naturally I'd missed hearing my name called again. I leapt up and in the glass case with the natural history specimens by the wall to the left, pale, with shocked eyes, the stranger loomed.

—Take your seat, the teacher said.

That winter I talked my classmates more than ever before. But I'd walk past Grete in silence. And she'd turn her head away as though she felt guilty. Still, hour after hour, the golden down of her nape shimmered before my eyes, gleaming over the frock of highest-quality British cloth that fit so matter-of-factly.

Anette was the chattiest creature in the class. She was always whispering something to Grete, and I'd see Grete's chiselled delicate profile lean towards her, astonished, aghast and—yes indeed, it was the very same expression she wore when he led her into church in her lily white wedding dress, the very same way I smiled last night under the cloying blue flowered lamp when I was sitting on Grete's sofa and he burst in through the door, that expression that turns a face a consuming shade of white like a bare sheet of paper shot through with invisible writing, that expression that knows nothing and betrays everything—oh, why don't I just say it: she smiled lewdly when Anette told her her stories. Lewdly, though ensconced like a precious object on the school bench, loved by her mother like life itself and raised in the light of immaculate milk-glass lamps.

Where Anette lived, there were only pot-bellied pink lamp-shades, decorative corncobs and pictures of angels on the walls, tatty satiny wallpaper and bloody linens in the tin bathtub. Anette's mother had a hair salon downstairs, where peroxide blonde girls gave spongy gentlemen manicures. Anette didn't have the money for sandwiches—Grete always ate wafer-thin white veal slices on wafer-thin rolls in the breaks—Anette owned a golden powder box hidden at the very bottom of her bag. Her skirts were a bit too short, her legs like inquisitive sticks, and when she laughed with her Chinese eyes, you saw all the teeth in her huge mouth. Her mother set great store by good breeding and every afternoon Anette went walking with a skinny Englishwoman.

I don't know how it came about, since Anette really didn't appeal to me at all, but one day I deftly prompted her with a Latin verb form, and that noon I walked home with my arm hooked through hers. Grete walked along beside us in a white fur hat, untouchable and indifferent. And all at once I had to tell Anette a 'secret'. A secret! Where's that supposed to come from at broad noon with the streetcars screeching and the air grey with dust? But a secret was what I felt compelled to tell. I clung tight to Anette, stuck my nose into her purple velvet coat that smelled of hair tonic and powder, and whispered:—Know what, I've done it already too.

Anette twinkled her roguish Chinese eyes, her mouth one great gaping red hole. To this day I don't know what she thought I meant, perhaps she had no more notion than I did. Anyway, she clamped my arm to her side, and I quickly added in a hoarse undertone:—But you mustn't tell a soul, not even—motioning my head towards Grete—her.

At lunch Mama said:—Why are you squinting your eyes that way? And Bea exclaimed:—Don't gape like that! I turned red. That was the secret. I didn't know what was behind it, but Anette knew. On the street Anette cocked her head when she went walking with her

Englishwoman, and gentlemen and errand boys stared after her. And when I went walking with my nanny in the afternoon, I cocked my head too, both inquisitive and indifferent, felt a pair of round little breasts come to life, and gazed at a man—I don't know what he looked like, maybe he had a red face, but he was a man, the first man in my life, though I loved Uncle Max so fervently.

And that night the pampered linen of my parental home turned grey and bristly beneath me, the nursery blanket over-warm, the room filled with smothering breath. And my fingers turned into tentacles, nasty red tentacles, slippery, strange to me, inquisitive fingers—Anette's fingers.

But the next day in the break Grete took me by the arm, and in the pane of an opened window with the chalkboard looming dark and menacing behind it, I saw the stranger's despairing scrutiny, terribly alien, more alien than ever.

Ulla had peculiar handwriting. Not too round, not too square, not too thin and not too thick, clear and assured, outstretched and self-contained. She printed the capital letters. The whole time I'd sat next to Grete, my exercise books were filled with the same childishly pointy, irregular letters. Grete's I's never lined up with their dots, and two or three times a week she'd try to write a hand that leaned steeply back, like a lady with perfumed stationery.

One day the teacher returned Ulla's German composition book with evident disapproval.—I wouldn't have expected work like this from you!

Ulla glanced inside. Her narrow mouth with its snowy, stumbling teeth gave a barely noticeable twitch. But when I got my composition book back, she silently took it herself and slid the other one over towards me.

The teacher had mixed up the books because I'd written in Ulla's handwriting. I was terribly ashamed. Like a thief. But Ulla didn't even mention it. That's the way Ulla was.

Really she was my first purely conventional acquaintance. All we ever spoke of was schoolbooks, pen holders and lesson plans. She had extraordinarily white wrists, translucent as porcelain, but coarse, chapped red hands. Supposedly she ran the household for her father and brothers. None of us had ever visited her at home.

One day Grete was missing. Anette turned around whispering, whispering to me and Ulla right in the middle of drawing class:— Her mother is very ill.

—My mother has been dead for years, Ulla said almost loudly with venom in her eyes. Those eyes always reminded me of water, blue, icy water. And it incensed me that Ulla had spoken so directly, so shamelessly. Why, Grete's mother—Grete's mother—a cloud of pink haze, shimmering lace and sweet security in milk-glass light. In milk-glass light, that's where Grete had to be. And the milk from her mother's broad good breasts was sweet—blossom-sweet.

Under the bench my legs went rigid and cold. I couldn't feel my shoes any more. All the strength and aliveness of my thighs converged on Grete's empty seat, I saw the golden down of her nape in front of me, the delicate line of her shoulders—

I thought of Uncle Max, how his hairy hand had clasped Grete's fingers, infinite fear for Grete seized me, cold, senseless fear, I stared at the black chalkboard, smooth and impenetrable as the lid of a coffin . . . .

A piercing bell rang. Break. Ten o'clock.

At 10 in the morning Grete's mother died.

The entire class went to the funeral. I felt wretched, for two days I'd hardly eaten a thing. When someone's dead, how can you eat?

It was a strange, torn pain that dogged me. A pain I was ashamed of. What was Grete's mother to me? I'd hardly known her. If only Bea didn't notice the state I was in.

It was as though I'd had a limb lopped off, something terribly alive. I saw Grete in front of me, missing an arm or missing a backdrop, sinking backwards into a dizzying void, I saw Grete lost on hazy streets, I saw her in a strange bed, sick and parched with fever.

And then I saw her for real, saw her black-veiled on her tall, handsome father's arm, crossing the graveyard threshold, following the coffin. It was a dazzlingly bright March day, the birds screeching like mad in the linden tree by the chapel, tulips and hyacinths growing on the graves, someone weeping, Anette giggling nervously and Ulla biting her thin lips. I stared at the coffin as it was carried along high up above us, draped in a black cloth.—

And suddenly I was all alone in the others' midst, amid the living, astir with whispers, and amid the wind-kissed tulips and hyacinths, oh Lord, I didn't even know the colour of the dead woman's hair, what her nose, her ears were like, and yet I was alone, dull and cast off like the coffin's dead wood, isolated, bereft, betrayed.

Because Grete was slender and lovely as she cast a clod into the open grave, blossoming in all her sorrow like an exuberant graveyard bloom. Even as she wept gentle tears, she never for a moment forgot that she was Grete, that all eyes were upon her, that the deep black set off her pale skin. She was unhappy, oh yes, of course, but a week later she'd laugh, a year later she'd dance—and there she stood, she, she alone, Grete, while a piece of her life sank away into the ground.

And she was a stranger to me, stranger than the girl in the mirror ever was. I nearly hated her.

In the streetcar I noticed that Ulla's frozen blue eyes were brimming with water. I edged up close to her, as far as possible from Anette, who was peering about, head cocked, eyes twinkling.—Are any of you coming to Grete's? she asked.—No, I said, and then I turned to Ulla:—Won't you help me with the maths exercise?—Then you'll have to come home with me, I've got an awful lot to do.

That was fine with me. Anything not to go home, where the afternoon sun was glaring on the grandfather clock, where Bea would ask:—How was it? and the maids would be sitting in the kitchen with their mending, lazy and poised for their evening off. And so for the first time I went home with Ulla.

Ulla lived in a low, squat house. Out front was a black yard with bare trees. Her father was a doctor. Even the stairwell smelled of ether and such like. There might have been a touch of iodine too. But the hallway with the faded red plush chairs and a table with ancient humour magazines (it also served as a waiting room) was so poor, so terribly poor that I flinched as though stabbed with an unsterilized hypodermic needle.

Ulla curled her lips. She wished she could send me away. Though I knew that, I followed her into the living room, where an operating chair stood in one corner by the window. I knew it, but I stayed.

That was sneaky, that was nasty of me. Altogether I'm definitely or very likely a terrible person. Inquisitive to an insane degree. A vampire. Just as right now I have to know how—yes, how he kisses, the way I have to savour everything the others know, back then I had to know where Ulla slept at night. It took just one look at the black leather couch.

I haven't changed. It was always the same thing. It started with Horky. Then came the others. Ulla too. A week ago, didn't I act exactly like her, pacing back and forth with him outside the house while upstairs Grete ran from room to room in her velvet-blue robe, tugging at the curtains and letting the tea kettle boil dry? But she knew to smile when he came up the stairs, smile with broad translucent teeth, just as I knew to smile when he phoned me this morning, knew to smile into the receiver, broad and bright, filled with sweet trust—Grete's smile.

Confound it—that smile had its effect. Grete's effect.

I'm a monster. Grete even thinks I'm a she-devil. She thinks I'm trying to snare her hus . . . —

And Anette thinks I'm a cold-hearted coquette, while Ulla thinks I'm a fond little goose.

The Devil only knows who's right.

The Devil—yes, maybe the Devil knows.

But I've got to get back, back, back to where I was! Otherwise there'll be a mess, the mess that mustn't be allowed, the primordial confusion that smothers everything, chaos and destruction.

So, I stood there in the parlour or consulting room, whatever you'd call it, and in the tall instrument cabinet by the wall between petri dishes and forceps stood the stranger. She was very dark. Or maybe the room was very dark. It got no light.

I wrenched myself around to face Ulla. Under the low ceiling she seemed as tall as though stretching up on purpose. Ready to jump, as though any moment she could leap out the window and into the world. The narrowness of these abject surroundings had made her feel such yearning that the muscles under her porcelain-pale skin were held in constant flowing tension. She wore her black hair even shorter than a boy's.

A moment later a boy walked into the room. He was her height, had the same hooked Jewish nose, but his skin was blemished by pimples. It was Ulla's younger brother.

She had two more brothers, but I never saw them. I'm sure all these brothers resembled each other.

So, Ulla's brother made a terribly awkward bow and after a few highly superfluous phrases immediately asked about Anette.

—He knows her from dancing class, said Ulla, pulling out a drawer in the black leather couch to rummage for her books.

—Swell girl, said Ulla's brother, smacking his lips. Evidently that referred to Anette. I found that awfully superfluous too, but I cocked my head and twinkled my eyes. At that moment Ulla turned on the huge unshaded bulb over the operating chair so she could see better. The light sliced into my eyes, caused sudden, terrible pain.

Ulla regarded me with her ice-water gaze:—Hurry up! I don't have much time. At that, I realized that she had to make dinner for these men she lived with, these strange men. Probably something copious and starchy. Her being so poor and all.

The spring that followed seems to have been awfully hot. Glaring bright as August and especially loud. The classroom windows were always opened wide, street noise rumbled into the Latin vocabulary, the mathematical theorems. The girls all wore filmy blouses, a bit sweaty under the arms. They suddenly acquired over-hefty breasts and sturdy hips, did callisthenics and danced in the breaks and smelled of stuffy fumes.

I can't have been much different, though I didn't know how I looked, anxiously shunning all mirrors, all shop windows, all glass panes with dark backgrounds. Grete had peculiar American shoes with little leather straps, and—she was a Protestant—had her religious instruction separately. Ulla wrote poems on her blotting paper, sonnets and tercets, strict forms and stark rhymes, but in between times she spent hours in parks, praying to pink horse chestnut blossoms, the laburnum's gold rain, or gnawed the iodoform-smelling pillow of her hard bed on the leather couch. She suffered from her youth as from a raging fever, while Anette had evening trysts in dark doorways with acne-scarred boys.

Meanwhile I was in love with Uncle Max, who came by nearly every evening. Bea had gotten engaged. With some *Herr von* . . . . He had gold spectacles, he was rich and owned a factory.

In the middle of all the heat and restiveness, Doctor Alexander arrived. Our old history teacher, who always spat all over the first row when he pronounced the dates, had died. And Doctor Alexander came in his place.

At the first lesson, everyone giggled. He was blond, too blond, really, and looked as though he'd just come from climbing a glacier. That was how brown he was. With yellow-smoked irregular teeth.

He impressed me no more than the janitor or the coal scuttles in the hall. But Grete's nape with the shimmering down struck me as astonishingly white, like chiselled marble against the background of the blackboard. And she was the first one he called on, and when she gave the wrong answer in her hoarse voice, he smiled. At which she took her seat, ladylike.

A few days later Ulla told Anette, harshly and ruthlessly right in front of me:—My brother cried last night. Why did you stand him up? Anette shrugged, twinkled her impudent Chinese eyes.—Listen, Ulla said warningly, I'm telling you, he's my brother.

At that moment Doctor Alexander walked into the classroom (looking back, it's as though we only ever had history class) and Anette slipped back to her seat. She had a new flashy green necktie on.

Ulla clenched her fists. My nails turned white.

Bea was going to be married soon. She and Mama spent all day putting together the trousseau. *Herr von . . .* stroked my cheeks and called me a little ladybug. One night I heard a strange noise in Bea's room. I got up and listened at the crack of the door. I felt as though I were rifling her dresser with the letters and photos.

Yes indeed, she was sobbing. Sobbing! Bea, the betrothed. Betrothed—what a ghastly word. I thought of *Herr von . . .*'s gold-rimmed glasses, how they always seemed spattered as if with fine toothpaste. I recalled his grey-striped trousers, had a sudden vision of a water closet in a strange hotel. Filled with horror, I crawled into bed. My nightshirt clung to me, wet with cold sweat.

But what did all that have to do with Doctor Alexander? It's not as though he could help Bea. Lately Grete was often absent, and he'd call on her and be dumbfounded that she wasn't there. Though he'd glanced over at her empty seat the moment he came through the door.

She lay in bed, the sun poured through the huge window, a pale-blue duvet warmed her cool weary body, on the nightstand a tiny alarm clock with silver hands ticked away and at 11 sharp Grete looked up with self-assuredly smiling broad teeth from the beautifully bound book she was holding. Now he was walking into the classroom, noticing her absence, calling on her . . . .

While I sensed Ulla's short breaths beside me, while I watched Anette quickly powder her inquisitive little nose. And Doctor Alexander, who'd just called on Grete in vain, now called on Ulla, Ulla, who always knew the answer; smiling, he leaned on the sill of the open window and it was as though Grete's soft-blue duvet was expanding endlessly over my body, filling my ears with wadding, choking my gorge with the odour of illness, and my stomach swelled, gigantic and menacing, stirred by life that wasn't mine, by strange limbs, water and blood—

Then Doctor Alexander called my name. And I replied in Grete's voice. Giving the completely wrong answer.

Oh God no, not that, that's the very thing I shouldn't have written. All I want is to tell what happened. I don't need to say yet what will be, what must never be.

You see, in those hours of school, when Grete lay in bed under the pale-blue duvet with reddened tonsils, quiet and dutiful, while Doctor Alexander missed her, in those agitated hours of life's first spring when Ulla wrote poems on blotting paper and Anette played with her golden powder box, everything, everything that I know is going to happen had happened already. For heaven's sake, is there no help for it! I, I, I, the one writing this book, this is me, isn't it—

I mustn't look up from what I'm writing. Because the window beside me reflects the desk lamp and sitting next to it, head bowed—the stranger!

Go on, go on writing! Write down how things were!

After that spring of Doctor Alexander, suddenly it was summer. Holidays. My parents had decided to take me and Bea to the North Sea. That *Herr von . . .* was going to join us there and the wedding would be held in autumn.

On the last day of school—it was so hot that Doctor Alexander taught class in his shirtsleeves, and even the director couldn't object, Doctor Alexander was wearing a grey-blue sports shirt—on the last day of school Grete looked as pale as the lilies the market women disembowel of their pollen so they won't make a mess. Though there are always a few yellow stains anyway. That's how pale Grete was. I leaned over to her, breathed in a faint yellowish smell of sweat, and for a moment it was as though her broad mouth with the translucent teeth would open to tell me that—

No, women like Grete don't speak, they never speak, even when they're little girls with no idea what they're carrying inside them. But her silence gagged me like a lump in my gorge, that certain special lump that's typical of hysterical women, as Ulla told me the other day—

Ulla, whose wrist was bandaged with yellow calico on that last day of school; she said she'd been bitten by a cat. And Anette took a velvet-red album up to Doctor Alexander's desk and had him sign it.—Address too, please, she said, and I was horribly embarrassed, because an album is for shopgirls, not for girls with higher education. But Anette sometimes kept kitschy German 'books for young ladies' in her desk.

—This summer will never end, said Ulla, when we shared a parting handshake on the street. The paving stones scalded the soles of our shoes. She went home to the cellar-cool house with the operating chair. Stayed there all that glaring summer . . .

Oh, that summer was the finest, the most incandescent of my life. Of my life, yes, that's right, for in truth this life of mine, already gnawed at by Horky's factory fate and Grete's mother's disembodied suffering, this life of mine, of my own, came to an end in that one splendid green-spuming salty North Sea summer. What remained was Grete, Ulla, Anette and maybe that stranger in her eternal mirrors, but as for me, I sank away all at once into the western sea with that blazing balloon, the sun, while the hotel guests ate lobster on the terrace—

I sank into the afternoon when Uncle Max vanished forever from my sight. Forever. Unimaginable. Un—im—agin—able.

I haven't seen him since.

Oh, it was so bright, I daresay it was much too bright. In the shimmering sand, billions of shells dazzled, the bracing waves when they cudgelled your back were bright, the wicker beach chairs were bright, the bathing machines in their trundling flight from the tides were bright, the frocks were bright, all the frocks, and the music from the bandstand. The nights were cool.

Bea and I slept in the same room. Her white stranger's body tossed and turned in bed by the opposite wall. Behind the window's high crossbars, a slender exquisite steeple stretched into the sky. Stars trembling around it.

And I couldn't close my eyes. The day's salty brightness danced around me in the narrow hotel room with its mahogany furniture. I suddenly saw that Bea had dazzling skin, and that she was lovely, lovely as the women in old pictures whose knights clapped them in chastity belts before setting off for the Holy Land.

I was very glad that she was my sister.

Yes, true, all those weeks I didn't think at all of Grete, Ulla, Anette, of school or Doctor Alexander.

It seems I was very happy, I changed my hairstyle. An English boy sat at the next table in the dining room. We took walks along the endless dunes to freshly washed, brightly painted Dutch towns.

Oh, the splendour of afternoons shimmering with shells!

No, it was impossible, utterly impossible that that *Herr von . . .* should ever come. He'd been expected for a week, but he didn't come, of course; in all this bright clarity he simply couldn't. Couldn't be allowed to. Because now I knew: He was stifling. Stifling in his wealth, his power that rustled like banknotes, stifling in his grey-striped trousers. I smiled to myself when Mama and Bea discussed his arrival. How could they fail to sense that he could never come here! How ludicrous!

Incidentally, Bea always talked about him like an item in her trousseau.

Meanwhile a postcard with an inkblot arrived. From Anette.—Do you know where He is? In Switzerland, in the Bernese Oberland.

I tossed the card into the library wastebasket.

Herr von . . . was coming. For certain. Today or tomorrow. Bea summoned the hotel hairdresser and quarrelled with the valet because her shoes weren't shined enough.

That evening, right in the middle of the glaring dining room, the head waiter suddenly pointed to our table. Bea started up. She'd gone red. (I'd never seen her go red before.) And Uncle Max came walking towards us.

He sat down at the table as though he'd just been to fetch his handkerchief. Yes, yes, passing through en route to England, two or three days, he expected.

I giggled to myself. Of course Uncle Max had to come, not that *Herr von* . . . . I'd show him my shell collection and—

Papa was sitting across from me. He had the same high, slightly hollow temples, the same slightly over-stiff back as Uncle Max, the same cautious way he'd move his elbows. Naturally, they were brothers, after all. Before now I'd never known that, I'd only ever heard it. But if Papa hadn't been so grey and old, so occupied by bank business and taking care of Mama and Bea—

Uncle Max, now, he'd take much better care of me, he'd know exactly what I need. With him I'd never need to feel ashamed. He'd understand how I can love a shell, an ordinary worthless shell in the sand.

I looked up at him. Naturally he was sitting next to Bea. His white fingers toyed with little balls of bread, and Bea looked at him bright-eyed as though he was why she'd summoned the hairdresser that morning. Her hair had a golden scent.

She was glad he'd come. And suddenly I knew not just that Papa and Uncle Max were brothers, but that Bea and I were sisters. We were kin to each other, terribly akin, and we'd been pushed as close together as though no air were left between our faces. Dishes clattered, a cork popped, Mama sat cool and distant between us, thinking perhaps of that *Herr von* . . .

And we were dangerously close . . .

What happened that night was my death. My early death. Before that I'd been the schoolmate of Grete, Ulla and Anette. But then—

One day the hour will draw near and one of them will come and take the pencil from my hand and go on writing—meanwhile Bea's happy with her *Herr von . . .* , meanwhile Bea has three children, three children from her *Herr von . . .* , and money, heaps of money, and silver and porcelain, all monogrammed with *von*.

My sister.

My God, where am I? The pencil's still clutched in my hand. The room is dark. Mahogany furniture. The steeple looms like an endless tapered finger outside the window with its high cross, a yellow moon pasted beside it, flat as cardboard, no air in between, between the steeple and the moon and the room and the mahogany furniture, between Bea's bed and my bed.

It goes without saying that Uncle Max came in. Once, abruptly, in the middle of the night, that night. It goes without saying that they thought I was asleep, or didn't think of me at all, I mattered far too little to them.

But all at once all my limbs blazed. My skin turned soft, all the warmth it had absorbed from the sea's green light gushed out into the hotel bed's thin coverlet. One wrench—and I was lying there stark naked, my prim child's nightgown torn down the middle—

The moon stuck to the windowpane, a meaningless yellow cardboard lid—and meaningless hot and hoarse voices. My voice was hot and hoarse too . . . . love you, someone said. Hot and hoarse.

No more air between us. Between me and Uncle Max. Between me and Bea. Bea and me.

For I was lying in his arms now, feeling the full incandescence of his famished kisses, soft hands full of kindred tenderness—Papa—Papa—won't you help me—my body, my pale, my ripe body reared up—what is this—oh God, I—I'm not wearing a chastity belt—why oh why are you kissing me—why oh—oh—oh.

The door closed abruptly with a creak of the latch, the room was filled with smoky haze, the steeple packed in rosy wadding, where on earth was I?

In my bed lay a gaunt brown parched child with a torn nightgown and a dry throat—the stranger.

And someone was crying. Bea. Or me. And every single chair seemed unreachably distant.

Next morning at breakfast—the burnished teapot reflected the white sun—a postcard was lying on my napkin. Ulla wrote: I'm cramming for the winter term—say, did you run off with my history book?

That afternoon Uncle Max departed. We accompanied him to the steamer.—I should be back soon. On the return trip. Maybe in a few days.

The siren wailed. In his right hand he held a gleaming black valise. The water seethed in numbing spume. The sea's green light was coldly blinding. Voices, fluttering handkerchiefs, sailors. Uncle Max waved one last time. I turned away. My eyes ached, they ached dreadfully.

I haven't seen him since that day. Haven't—seen—him—since.

That evening *Herr von* . . . was sitting at our table next to Bea. He called me a ladybug and Bea smiled. Naturally she smiled. Naturally she had to marry him. You mustn't marry blood relatives, or you might have blind children. I'd read that in a novel.

The next day, stormy and rainy, I held a postcard from Grete in my hand: I'm looking forward to school again. Do you think we'll still have the same teachers?

I stared out into the clouds' raging tatters—Grete's gentle downy nape, Doctor Alexander, Ulla's cold eyes in her porcelain-hard face and Anette's little powder box—

Uncle Max was gone. Bea got married to that *Herr von* . . . .

And I belonged with them again, just as I belong with them still.

Today, yes today, that was an awful day just now. I was coming from work—it's a good thing all I deal with is books, if they were people, I'd knife them, though surely I'm not a murderess, no surely not.

Now Ulla, she could slip cyanide into someone's morning coffee as a matter of conviction, and Anette would do it offhand, by afternoon she'd have forgotten, at most she'd twinkle her eyes—

Grete, though, would never stoop to that.

Oh Lord, what am I babbling on for, I meant to write about today, though that's all wrong, I wanted to go one thing at a time, and I was only just writing about Doctor Alexander—the name's Axel now and he's a professor, as if that mattered, as if it mattered in the slightest!

Really I just keep writing the same thing, the same old story from our school days, the same story, always following the same pattern—and that pattern is me, Grete, Ulla and Anette.

I think I'm pining for Uncle Max.

And maybe I'm pining for Horky, too.

So, I was heading home from work—like she always does when something utterly intolerable has happened, the stranger's crouching in the mirror again, I'm going to turn that mirror to the wall—heading from work with dusty hands, it was nearly lunchtime, drizzling, and in front of the university I happened to see him. The moment I was about head towards him, he smiled and waved at me, imperiously, matter-of-factly, as though I were his wife—

Me, his wife—where did he get that idea!

Ulla would never put up with that sort of thing, naturally, she's self-reliant, working as an assistant, someone who signs prescriptions.

Even Anette wouldn't let herself be waved at like that, though all she does is sing low-down songs in her metal-string voice.

So, he waved to me, I went up to him, in a moment he'll ask if the soup's served, the soup! My nostrils filled with a warm meat smell, hints of celery and leek, I felt sick, I turned away, ran home, had to vomit on my way up the stairs—

Oh God, that's impossible, all we did was kiss, awful, devouring, frenzied, biting, bloody kisses . . . .

—All you have to do is kiss a lot, and that makes the babies come, Anette told me once a long time ago. It was between lessons, she was wearing a black school pinafore embroidered in red, her lips were red, she was sucking on a red lozenge, I believe, and she was so short that when she washed the blackboard, she had to climb on a chair to reach the top with the wet sponge.

She was class monitor that week.

All that is utter nonsense, and it's totally superfluous for me to be remembering it today.

Unlike the story of the girl who came to see Ulla's father.—It started with the soup, it always made me sick, she said, that's how it was the first time, that's how I knew right away.

It was winter and very cold, it was right before that oh-so-nasty trick, ah yes, that's right, it was Doctor Alexander's last year, and I was grown-up enough to understand everything, everything, everything.

I came to Ulla's place, probably about another maths problem or something like that, because I always needed some excuse to visit. She'd look at me then with ice-water eyes that knew everything, knew exactly how inquisitive I was, about the black leather couch, the glaring light bulb over the operation chair, the acne-scarred brother.

That afternoon the yard with its black knotted trees lay under a stifling fog of snow. Cloudy wadding shot with pink. It clogged up your throat.

When I walked through the waiting room with the faded red plush furniture, the girl was perched on the edge of an armchair in a black coat, fumbling with the stained humour magazines.

Ulla dragged me straight into her brother's room, a blue-striped mattress on the floor, the cast-iron stove fuming, a drawing board with the compass still stuck in it leaning against the wardrobe. And before I could open my mouth, the key turned in the door to the consulting room—or was it the dining room?—and we were locked in the narrow room with the three camp beds.

None of that would have seemed the least bit suspicious if Ulla hadn't suddenly looked like our nanny did the time she stole Mama's earrings. She sat slouched on the mattress, her face gleamed like a white stone in the rosy twilight, a branch stretched like a stout black arm outside the window, and Ulla talked and talked, even talked about Doctor Alexander, which she never did otherwise. But still I overheard the story about the meat broth.

I was afraid, I shut my eyes, thought of knitting needles, long cruel metal needles—then nothing but whispers—someone moaned

. . . .

I left as soon as the door to the operating room was unlocked. The huge bare bulb blazed over the white chair, the plush armchairs in the hall were disarranged, humour magazines lay on the floor, the girl was gone and out on the street big melting flakes floated through the grey winter air.

The next day Ulla was late to history class. Her narrow lips were swollen, as if they'd been bitten. She'd stuck a newspaper in her atlas—and I opened my eyes wide, felt them freeze in a blue ice-water stare, my hands lengthened, trembled.

I read:

. . . . . . around 7 in the evening . . . . . the waitress G. E. . . . . suddenly collapsed with haemorrhages . . . . . . taken to the hospital . . . . illegal operation————refused to speak . . . . around midnight . . . . dead.

G. E. . . . . Ulla knew, I knew . . . . that G. E. was the girl with the meat broth. There she'd been, fumbling with the humour magazines. G. E. . . . What could her name have been? Gisela, Gertrud, Grete—no, surely not Grete, but maybe Genofeva or even Griseldis.

Horky's already got a daughter, a big girl. A daughter with sparse blonde hair and old working hands, a girl everyone grabs under the smoking brick chimneys—

Heavens above, who'll help this girl!

And who'll help me, who can help at all! I still have the smell of that broth in my nose, lunchtime today in front of the university, I had to vomit in the stairwell—Or was it a bathroom with white tiles, toilet water and a cork mat? Wasn't I wearing a—a pale velvet robe over—over—

No, no, no! That wasn't me. And that's the last thing I ought to be writing about. I, I, I loved Uncle Max, I'm a librarian with a steady salary, even a pension fund, I, I went to school with Grete, Ulla and Anette, I too must have had history with handsome Doctor Alexander, he had a mountain tan and yellow-smoked teeth, I was the one who played the nasty trick, who betrayed the others—

And even if I know a thousand times over what they went through, even if I've felt it a thousand times, still I was the murderess (murderess in a small way) and they were the victims.

My victims!

All that happened because I loved him. That is to say: Did I really love him? I don't know. I don't know.

And even today I don't know if I love him. That's what's so weird, that's what's so dangerous.

Because if I, I could walk up to him today and say:—Come with me to Spain or New Zealand—how simple that would be, how matter of fact! He wouldn't come, of course, he wouldn't dream of it, but then I'd have an unhappy love affair and that would be good too.

As it is, though, I smile, I smile like Grete, gently and with broad maternal teeth, he tells me about his work as though I had Ulla's crystal-clear mind, and sometimes I suddenly bat my eyes, bat Anette's Chinese eyes until he reaches for me, as if—as if I were a streetwalker someone frequents.

But the stranger girl's at my side, in a polished windowpane somewhere, in a pitcher of water, recently I even saw her in the glass of his watch face, and she never looks at him. She doesn't love him, I daresay, she wants no part of him.

Now, where've I got off to again? Today—yes today—

None of this has any business here, it doesn't belong here at all. I have no intention of telling some complicated love story with betrayal and adultery and that sort of thing. I'm just recounting my childhood, my youth, its agonies, its struggles, its errors, and if all that's set down here, possibly even printed black on white, I mean literally black on white, then, isn't it so, then there'll be no more doubt that these were really my agonies, my struggles and my errors.

Because I, isn't it so, I also have a right to life, my life, even if it keeps trickling away between my fingers like water. I love the sea.

The whole class had a crush on Doctor Alexander. It was perfectly simple: he was a man. He didn't have gout or varicose veins or evening card games, nor a wife with hair pinned up in pigtails like the other teachers. He was handsomest on Mondays. Because on Sunday he'd have taken a nice long ski trip, and when the door opened in front of him a breeze like mountain air would blow in and the classroom would smell of snow. It also smelled a wee bit of sweat, of stables and wool, but the girls didn't notice that. Grete sat there as though she were all grown up, as though her husband had died, she had three children to provide for and was awaiting Doctor Alexander's advice. Ulla thrust out her lower jaw—she did that when she was thinking hard. About Joanna the Mad and the conquest of Mexico, or also about the girl G. E.? Ulla always knew everything. Whereas Anette giggled, gave the wrong answers, mixed up the centuries and sat down again gratified when she'd managed to make him laugh. Then he'd pass his handkerchief over his face as if to blow his nose, and everyone would be furious. Only I couldn't help laughing too. A tickling slippery laugh that I struggled to bite back.

It was a filthy day, the snow melted on the windowpanes, the roofs were grey, people waded down the streets as though through viscous chocolate. If the sun had been shining, I would hardly have played the nasty trick. It was a Monday, incidentally, just before the end of the semester.

The week before, under Doctor Alexander's lectern, Anette had found a notebook of his where he'd written down the seven questions for the final written exam.

That Sunday afternoon, she invited us over with great ceremony, served us whipped cream with spoons in a little room as pink as a layer cake with pictures of angels, amid a vile smell of brilliantine and burned hair because her Mama's 'salon' was right next door, and she read the questions out loud. Ulla was indignant and said it was cheating, Grete said for shame, but when she heard that the notebook had telephone numbers and a name in it too, she had a look after all.

I wasn't interested in the phone numbers or the name, but I stayed up all night cramming for history. And then that filthy Monday came.

When the exam was over, Grete was bright red, Ulla bit her nails and Anette had a smoke in the lavatory. Suddenly I said:—Well then! and followed Doctor Alexander into the staff room. I did, me, all by myself! I went up to him at the green baize table, a bit apart from the other teachers, feeling very big, gigantic in my perfidy, as though I weren't alone, as though someone else, a stranger were inside me.

And then I told him.

Traitor!

He pushed his horn-rimmed glasses up his nose, turning bright red and awfully flustered, I saw that his brown skin was filled with big pores, and I added:—I was the one who found the notebook, but all four exams are invalid.

He turned away:—Well, we'll talk about it later, he stammered, and left me standing there. I went into the classroom and told the others.

Grete cried, she cried big, pale, lukewarm tears, Ulla clenched her fists and said:—You must have gone out of your mind, and Anette stamped her feet. I saw that her nails were long, pointed and polished, and I thought she'd sink them into my face, my eyes.—Why not go and write it on the blackboard too! Ulla jeered. No, that's not what I did. I sat down very quietly on my seat, my knees trembled, the ground vanished underfoot, I sank into brown snow, chocolate-coloured street muck—

The golden down on Grete's upright nape—Doctor Alexander despised her—Ulla's ivory wrist, atremble with blue veins—Doctor Alexander didn't even bother to go over her exam now—Anette's half-open moist red mouth—His notebook had a name in it, and several phone numbers . . . .

It was so sad.

Sad, too, that Doctor Alexander never mentioned the whole thing again. Not to us, not to the director. There was no scandal. And that was the saddest thing. All of that and all of us weren't the least bit important to him.

That oh-so nasty trick—a mere nothing now, almost laughable. And Doctor Alexander lost his lustre. He'd become a man like you'd encounter any day on the street. Why talk about him, think about him? He was sun-burned, but his face had big pores. Teeth that were far too smoke-stained. Oh, fiddlesticks!

Grete and her father went off to the Riviera for two weeks. Anette strolled in the park with Ulla's brother again, Ulla read Schopenhauer, and soon they'd forgiven me. The whole foolish business wasn't worth mentioning.

Altogether you couldn't take school seriously for long. When even Doctor Alexander didn't take it seriously.

Oh, yes, I'd played an awfully nasty trick. We'd become adults, suddenly, in a single day. We'd learnt not to take love seriously. Us four. Grete, Ulla, Anette and I.

That spring Mama fell ill. Just before that Bea had gotten married, very grandly, but I don't want to write about it, it was just too revolting.

Mama was ill, very ill, in fact, and suddenly I wasn't just the little girl who only comes in to say good night, because her big sister takes care of everything, suddenly I was the daughter who had to minister to Mama—the daughter!

I sat by Mama's bed, oh, the conjugal bed, the window open on account of her congestion, her face, otherwise so pallid and always serene, was red and agitated. Outside the rain came down, a lukewarm endless rain, the lilacs were fragrant, already rotting on the bush—and I knew that Mama was going to die. Not today, not now, there was nothing wrong but what was bound to be wrong with a woman her age, the doctor said, bound to be, just as one day you're bound to die—

Grete's mother had lived like someone with no legs and today Grete was dancing at a rainy spring party.

Ulla's mother had perished giving birth to her youngest son.

Anette's mother had hair dyed cinnabar red.

And my mother—

Warmth came between my thighs. A dark, a muffled, an enigmatic aching life flowed away beneath me, flowed into the damp ground, the dark, the muffling ground.

A cow lies heavy in the grass beneath an apple tree in bloom—the cornflower-blue quilt lies soft and rumpled on Mama's bed, on Papa's bed.

All the agonies of the first night come to life again, agonies of accidental births, lonely dusks—

Mama, Mama!

Horky had six children, six or maybe seven. Her breasts had dangled heavy. Milk-glass light shone on Grete when she came into the world, a nursemaid awaiting her in a nursery all painted white, while Ulla was tossed into the clothesbasket, a shrieking red bundle, and Anette was born in a maternity ward where the women all had to wear blue-and-white striped gowns. A nun had taken delivery of her.

Once, as my suckling eyes still stared at the ceiling, Uncle Max had gazed at me a long, long time.

Soon, Bea was going to have that *Herr von . . .*'s child.

I've gone mad, gone mad for sure, not even this book will help me. The moment I write the word child, 'child', that smell is back, the meat broth, a fat onion floating in it, what have I, I got to do with meat broth!

No, that was the girl. G. E. was her name. Genofeva or Griseldis. But me, I'm not a Griseldis. I'll never stand there in a blue velvet robe putting the kettle on, putting the kettle on over and over while he's waiting for Ulla on some street corner.

Yesterday I saw them together. Ulla walked along beside him indifferently, her hands in her coat pockets. Why shouldn't she? That sort of thing doesn't matter much to her. Even back in school she'd resolved to divide her life into compartments. She's too clever to wait. She's too clever altogether.

And if he picks up Anette outside the theatre tomorrow or the next day and they vanish into an automobile—Anette's got a white fluffy fur coat—well then, Ulla will shrug, her colleague Doctor N. N. lives next door at the clinic. Ulla's clever, Ulla will go next door. With Grete meanwhile expecting her first child.

Oh, there's no way, there's no point, I can't go on writing. Every time I write the word child—

Do I even have to write that word at all?

I'm never going to mention any child again. The stranger doesn't have a child either.

Incidentally, the stranger was never one of us four. She always stood off to the side, merely watching. Watching is a sneaky thing altogether. Who has the right to watch other people!

Sometimes at night when I open my window, especially in the summer, the stranger looms up to stare at me—as though sprouting up from strange depths.

That's why I don't like to sleep with the windows open. Though Ulla thinks that's uncivilized. She sleeps with open windows even when it's ten below, she doesn't care if her temples ache in the morning.

But watching, just looking, examining the world like a bug through a magnifier, not knowing what the other person's feeling, feeling, suffering, wanting—

I can't do that. Won't ever be able to.

Not even in the theatre. I had an awful experience once at the ballet. After that spring when I'd spent so much time at Mama's bedside. She took me to the opera house, she always did when Papa was away. She didn't like to, though.

It was very hot and a lady in front of us with a flabby back was wearing a lily-of-the-valley perfume that smelled all yellow and a bit like crumbled leaves. They were doing a common-or-garden ballet, sugar-sweet music with pink legs, pointe shoes and pasteboard bushes hung with nets. The ballerina in the third row on the left was sugar-sweet as well, with curly doll's hair and a hairdresser's smile, she looked just like she was supposed to, only that her legs weren't quite what they ought to be, not curvy enough, no calves. They were more like long straight sticks, slender branches, lopped off smoothly from a noble trunk.

I stared at those legs. They shimmered white under the pink stockings. I felt infinitely weary. My eyes fell half-shut. All I saw was those legs, completely white now, milky, a little grey room, a washbasin of grey water with powder floating pink on the surface, banknotes on the wooden table, a potted azalea and in the dressing table drawer a photo torn to bits. . . . .

Garish applause, the ballerina in the third row on the left spins on her toe, blows kisses to the audience—but what I see is a glass of water, a teeny bilious-green powder box.

She smiled with white teeth like a toothpaste advert, and I saw it clear as day: her face was like a skull.

The woman with the flabby back took the lily-of-the-valley handkerchief out of her beaded bag and blew her nose with a loud snort.

Should I call the police, the ambulance brigade, go to the director, have them rescue the girl, should I—

In the cloakroom Mama said to me:—Do come on now. You're always such a bore. Yes, a bore.

Now Grete, she was never a bore. In those same months the world opened up before her, a wide, white-cobblestoned, morning-sunny world. And it was her father who flung open the nursery door for her.

Summer full of sails, railroad trains with velvet seats, Chinese lanterns strung beneath chestnut trees. Iced lemonades and a band going mad on the bandstand.

Grete swam out into blue expanses. Breathing slowly and evenly, with the calm, confident pace of a dutiful pupil attentive to her swimming teacher's lessons.

And everyone watched. Her father's students sitting in his lectures, taking notes in the auditorium, watched her go up or down the stairs. Ladies admired her through lorgnettes when she danced in her pale summer frocks, danced the tango with confident, swaying, measured steps.

Oh gentle waiting, free from impatience!

Her father's first assistant had a white high forehead. Eyes with a bit of a stare, so pale that they were practically colourless. When he said 'Fräulein Grete', his hands turned moist. Big hands with white feeble fingers. Sickly hands. And he had bluish sickly teeth.

One Sunday afternoon he strolled with her across a meadow filled with daisies. Bells pealed. Around her neck she wore a thread-thin gold chain. And her frock was forget-me-notblue.

It was so warm—not hot; so bright—not glaring. She was thinking of the roast she'd ordered, the wine she'd had cooled, the fruit, the flowers on the table—lowering her head, she felt something wet and cold on her nape, where the golden down began—the assistant's lips.

He'd turned blood red.—Fräulein Grete, forgive me—I love you—I adore you—Never, never again—

He was gone, he'd vanished in the glinting beech thickets. Grete's knees trembled. Slowly she wiped the back of her hand on her forget-me-not-blue summer frock. She felt slightly ill.

She went to bed. A headache. Shutters closed, she lay between fresh cool sheets.

So that was love. Maybe he was going to go drown himself. No, hopefully not, that would be too tragic. Would he write her a letter? Ah, that wouldn't be so bad, just as long as there weren't any kiss, never again a wet, slippery kiss.

Something pained her, a faint and slightly agreeable pain.

The next day when the assistant greeted her she gave a stand-offish nod. He wrote her a despairing apology. She left it unanswered. He packed and left. She wept resentful tears for half an hour before bed. She thought he'd come back. He didn't come.

Oh silent waiting, free from dreams!

Of course, I knew all about it by the time she was sitting back in front of me in class. We were grown-up girls now. Sixth formers. I could practically smell it in the down of her nape, furious that she'd never tell me anything—when it came to things like that, Grete never talked to anyone, not even to herself—and I hated her, knowing he wasn't even worthy of touching her frock.

That forget-me-not blue summer frock.

Meanwhile that same summer I'd slapped a foolish boy good and proper behind a hedge once. There'd been a long prelude, with letters on lined paper, and one time he ambushed me when I—

But really, it's not worth mentioning, utterly without interest. Why write it down!

Ulla, though, that could never happen to her, someone sneaking up behind or her nape getting—

For years now she'd stood poised as on a swaying trampoline, and not until she told herself:—Ready, set, go! would she leap into a love story, a night of despair or a human heart.

With Ulla, everything was so uncertain, so dependent on the whims of chance and her mood.

Incidentally, before I forget, that last year of school we didn't have Doctor Alexander any more. That is to say, it wasn't that important, really, no one even thought to mention it. Only Anette said:—Too bad! I was soooo in love with him, meanwhile drawing a cinnabar-red line over her moist overlarge upper lip. That summer little Anette had grown quite a bit.

Ulla had gotten skinny, awfully skinny. Her porcelain-white skin had taken on a yellow tinge. Probably from all the swimming she did. Incidentally, she'd won a prize in her swimming club.

Impatient, that's what Ulla was. Her blue ice-water gaze flickered. Maybe there was snow in it, melted ice floes.

Her oldest brother began to pick her up from school now and then. He was better looking than the boy with the pimples, very tall, spasmodically lithe with Ulla's sharp nose. He never seemed to see the other girls; when Ulla came he'd take her books and turn away at once.

I remember one time Anette stuck out her tongue behind his back. Thank goodness Ulla didn't notice.

Because she loved him dearly, more than she loved her father, who resembled a rabbi with his silky beard and his silky voice, more than her other brothers, the incorrigible louts. He was someone she could ask for advice. He'd just finished his studies and was working at a children's hospital. She wanted to study medicine and wear a white coat too.

He had a friend. I saw that friend just one single time on a chance visit to that squat house. And I don't know whether I'm remembering right or imagining things: His name was Hermann. Yes, of course, it had to be Hermann, I'm sure of it.

He was just as tall as the oldest brother, also a doctor at a children's hospital, with the same shy, stand-offish way of offering his hand. The sight of his brown hair made me think of olives, caustic-salty, meltingly oily olives.

He didn't even look at me, couldn't look at anyone with his overlong lids that drooped over his eyes. It was repulsive, really.

Ulla talked to him just like she did to her oldest brother, curtly, familiarly, with a show of indifference:—Do you want coffee? No, not those cigarettes, try these, they're better.

It must have been awfully hard on Ulla not to have a mother.

And if Mama had taken a bit better care of me, it never would have crossed my mind to fall for Uncle Max so young and so hard.

Three days a week Ulla had gymnastics, three days she went swimming, she took jujitsu, and Sunday after Sunday she went on gruelling climbing trips with her oldest brother and Hermann.

She read a great deal, tough books she couldn't digest in those sleepless nights.

Once, as they descended into a valley on a golden October afternoon, she asked him:—Why won't you do it? You know how much I need it.

Hermann looked at her. She was wearing trousers, her hair was cut like a boy's, deep-black purple leaves rustled underfoot. His lids lowered.

—Nonsense, Ulla. You're too young.

—Not a bit. But you're afraid because I'm a girl.

Bouncing pebbles. Ulla's brother came bounding after them. White mist rose from the brown crags like smoke.

And then they came to a church, some village church where evening prayers were being held. In the farmyard next door, grapes were being pressed, yeasty juice smells mingled with the incense; rosaries and prayerful headscarves, murmurs beneath sweet long shining candles—

And they grabbed each other's hands in the shadow of the columns, three lost children from an infinitely far, vast and sultry land. Three siblings. Dark and desirous in their touristic hair shirts.

The next day Ulla told me everything, well, not about the church, of course, not about the mist and the purple beech leaves. That's the sort of thing you know on your own. All she described was a night in a spartan student room, a night of pain and sheltering arms, torment and release . . . .

And it smelled—we were sitting on a damp bench in an autumn-damp park—all around me it suddenly smelled of salt and olive oil, the brown trunks blurred before my eyes, everything turned brown, with one single bloody rupture—

—What's the matter with you? Ulla asked. How can anyone be so squeamish? It was a very good and sensible thing, maybe not very nice, but necessary.

How clever she was! Far, far too clever. But I gazed up at her and imbibed a new, sweet light, a rosy light from her severe ice-water eyes.

I felt buoyant that day. Even maths, which I always had such an awfully hard time with, didn't cause me any headaches. And when Bea and that *Herr von . . .* dropped by that evening, I gave him my hand as though, well, as though he weren't my sister's husband, but just *Herr von . . .*, a stranger who didn't concern me.

Oh, we shouldn't to be able to remember, shouldn't take such pleasure in remembering it all. We should slough off the days like old clothes, give them away, discard them, burn them—they belong on the rubbish heap! And never, never should we wear other peoples' clothing.

I oughtn't to have done it, never had the right to. There I go, writing the story of Ulla's first love—maybe it wasn't even her first love, maybe it wasn't love at all.—Oh, fiddlesticks, it was a golden crystal-clear autumn, in the evening warm mists stole into the houses, people sat together under veiled lamps, Hermann's eyes were veiled, overlong lids hung down over them, veiling me, no, Ulla, or maybe me too—

At any rate, I was happy as I described that autumn yesterday, sitting alone in my room with six sharpened Koh-i-Noors and gleaming paper, without the stranger.

And then today I did a foolish thing and went to Grete. Just because he'd written me a postcard about a stupid book.

It's already plainly visible—the child, that is. Grete's long brown eyes have lost their reddish light, they're dull as packing paper. And her lips over the broad prim teeth are chapped.

I can't go on writing about the old days any more, however much I'd love to linger over Ulla and that autumn when we turned eighteen.

Of course I mentioned Ulla today, Grete was pouring tea, wearing a yellow morning gown, not listening, and he said: Ah yes, Ulla, she's clever, much too clever.

Just yesterday I wrote the same thing myself. Yes, really, there it is, black on white. Isn't that crazy.

And it's crazy that he draped Grete's raincoat over my shoulders because of the rain. And that he escorted me. He needn't have done that, even if I was wearing Grete's raincoat. And he walked along beside me, and it was raining, and the streetlamps swam in yellow blots on the swimming dark pavement, he held up the umbrella, I slipped my arm through his—

And when we reached my home, outside the front door, he kissed me on the mouth, a big jolly kiss. He didn't even care if anyone saw—just a quarter of an hour ago, it was—and I responded to that kiss with a slight twitch of my lips, as matter-of-fact as if it were a train station, and we an old married couple.

And here I sit with Grete's raincoat hanging in front of the window, waterproof, best quality, the arms dangle gentle and sad and I don't dare to turn around, because that's not the stranger in the dark pane, oh God, if only it were!

No, what's aswim in that pane is a broad smile, a good smile, a maternal smile with chapped lips—

At my nape I feel the curl of golden down.

I shan't write any more today.

So, meanwhile several days have passed. Not nice days, not pleasant days. My head, my hands and feet were heavy, I even stayed home from the library once, kept thinking of peaches and yellow grainfields.

And twice I tried to write. But I had such a clumsy stupid adolescent scrawl and the paper went swimming sky blue across the table and suddenly turned into a letter to him. It's better if we stop seeing each other and that sort of thing. I tossed that letter into the coal hod. It looked so unnatural.

Today I met Anette. She told me—yes, well, right now I'm not going to put down what she told me. Let's go back, back to the days when I was eighteen, Grete went to balls and ran the household for her father, Ulla took daredevil ski tours with her brother and Hermann and Anette got kicked out of school.

If Anette hadn't got kicked out of school, a lot of things would have turned out differently. No one ever found out the reason. But I knew, of course I did. Because I always went to her mother to have my hair washed. The 'salon' was for ladies and gentlemen. In the middle was a red rayon curtain with bouquets of flowers that squirmed like tentacles.

Anette's mother took care of me herself. Because I went to school with Anette, because I was her friend. She hoped I'd be a good influence.

Oh, Anette was supposed to have it better than her mother. No salon with a rayon curtain, burned hair, shaving soap and rosy manicurists for her. Anette had gotten an education, was supposed to become self-reliant.

Self-reliant! Anette's mother had cinnabar hair and lots of gold teeth. Her bosom bounced when she towelled your hair dry, she quarrelled with the girls and most of all with Anette, who loitered around near the curtain with fashion magazines propped on her knees instead of doing her homework. But whenever the fat hairdresser said 'self-reliant', then her face—a funny face really, with a preposterous pug nose—her face would turn reverent—like Horky's when she talked about a posh movie theatre—and all of a sudden she'd shriek:—That creature's got to get out, that creature's yanking at the curtain again! She'd brandish a hairdryer as a glittering sword, and Anette would strut out the back door on her inquisitive legs that still reminded me of sticks, her Chinese eyes smiling indulgently.

Of course, Anette was determined not to go on with cheap stockings forever hiding her long stick-legs with their yellowish jungle skin. Or with lipstick that tasted of red bugs. And in the locker room before callisthenics, I saw she was wearing a Crêpe-de-Chine slip edged with zig-zag lace. She raised her finger with its pointed manicured nail to her swelling lips: Shhh, don't tell anyone! I know I can rely on you.

No, no, you can't rely on me, that's just the thing. Everyone thought they could, and that's why it's all going wrong. They entrusted me with everything, their joys, their agonies, their love, their hatred, their desires and, one time, even a gold pocket watch.

That watch was disgustingly fat. It was right before Christmas, and Anette came running to me with it. I was packing various presents in colourful tissue paper when she burst into my room, and though it was getting dark already, I distinctly saw that she was green in the face, green as wobbling seaweed, and her lips were bare and moist and unmade-up.

—Hey, she said breathlessly, I can rely on you (that again)—here, take this to the pawn office for me. I need money. For Christmas, of course. Well, don't I—

And off she went. Amid the Christmas presents on a pile of tissue paper lay the watch. As I said, it was a fat watch, with a fat gold rim, fat little hands and fat numbers.

I couldn't touch it. I wanted to, I tried. Impossible. I stared at it. Whispering dusk.

A grey sheet—hairy hands—blunt fingers—toothless lust—Anette's legs—kicking sticks—jungle sticks—and a nightstand with a grey marble top—the chamber pot by the bed—the watch on the grey marble top, alongside the handkerchief and the wallet, the golden, fat watch . . .

I felt violently ill. But Mama called me to dinner. And the watch was still lying there on top of all the tissue paper. Then I did the stupidest thing I possibly could: I took a sheet of tissue paper I'd set aside for its sweet doll-pink hue and wrapped the watch in it.

That colour was probably why the pawn office official suspected me, and the police showed up before I'd even tucked the money away, all that money, surely enough for a whole new wristwatch, the thin, flat kind with a ring of tiny brilliants—

By then I was already under arrest.

Typical, said the police officer as I stood in front of his desk and he took down my statement. I balled up my handkerchief, shifted my weight from leg to leg, and with them acting so awfully solemn about a watch, a fat gold watch, I had to giggle, just a little bit, squinty-eyed.

Then a lady came from welfare or whatever it's called and hauled me over the coals. It was no good. I knew nothing whatsoever. Nothing about the gold watch and nothing about any Herr Neumann—

that was his name, you see. I just kept talking about the pink tissue paper and the lady got very angry and said I was godless and hopelessly depraved. Now I really had to laugh, and who knows what might have happened if an officer hadn't suddenly come in and cleared the whole thing up. Because meanwhile Herr Neumann had phoned to say that he'd managed to find his Anette.

I was sent home.

Papa was in despair, he wrung his hands and said I was harming his reputation, but I didn't care. Nor did I even care that Mama was crying. I'd always thought she wouldn't cry over me unless I died. But I was glad that Uncle Max had vanished. I'd have been hideously ashamed in front of him.

—You're such a fool, Papa said.

A fool—he was probably right about that. Certainly, it was foolish of me to keep thinking all the while of the hairdresser with the cinnabar mane. Because now Anette had gotten kicked out of school right before the final exams, now she couldn't 'become self-reliant'. Self-reliant—what was that supposed to mean? It meant no money from Papa or any other man.

And I went to see Anette's mother and she was awfully nice, not angry at all. Though I'd made such a mess of things. She sat me down right there and washed my hair—come on now, you're a sight to see!—and then she told me that she'd been a fallen girl, a high-tone concierge had seduced her, and after that, well, after that she'd never been self-reliant again. And she wanted to spare Anette that fate and that's why she sent her to our school.

She had to yell awfully loud, because she was drying my hair with the hairdryer, and kept peering into all the mirrors to make sure no one else was in the salon. It was Sunday morning.

When suddenly Anette emerged from behind the red curtain with the tentacles. She was wearing a brand-new wristwatch, one of those thin, flat ones with a ring of tiny brilliants.

Then her mother started crying, Anette's mother, the cinnabar hairdresser, and she wouldn't take any money for washing my hair.—After all, today is Sunday.

Ulla was outraged that they'd simply gone and kicked Anette out. A violation of personal liberty was what she called it. And for the next few days she demonstratively strolled around with her right in front of school.

But Grete flushed slightly when people talked about Anette. When really she'd been her closest friend, she'd sat next to her for years, ever since that memorable autumn day when she'd suddenly moved to sit apart from me. She'd whispered with Anette, listened to Anette's 'secrets', but listen was all she did, women like Grete never speak, they never say a word—their voices are hoarse, and maybe their hearts are hoarse as well.

Recently Grete told Ulla what a beautiful, what an incredibly beautiful thing pregnancy is. How divine, how exalted you feel.

Can you feel exalted when you're nauseous? When you're vomiting?

Surely Horky never felt exalted, much less divine, in any of her eight pregnancies, it was eight, I think, once or twice it fell through.

And beautiful—Is it beautiful to have a big belly, dumpy legs and rings under your eyes?

No, I don't think so, and he doesn't think so either. I sensed that in the park the other day when he ran his eyes over my hips. Since I started doing Swedish callisthenics with Ulla, I'm acquiring hips like hers, steeply sloping hips that keep pace with your legs when you walk quickly and surely.

I feel his eyes run over my hips and it makes me think of a journey, of a ship with tall, shining white sails.

It's good for me to write this book, above all it's important, because now I realize how bad I am, how nasty. I want to have him, love him, I'm in love with him, thirsting for him, I know he wants to reach out and grasp me—the way men grasp Ulla when she slips off her white lab coat and stretches out her long strong arms—and he wants to toss me down on a bed, on some couch somewhere, the way a person like Anette gets tossed down, at some point or other—but I want to bear a child, his child—like Grete.

Oh, us four! When we'd passed our final exams—Ulla did a grand job, Grete quite pathetic, but the professors smiled at her in her gentle beauty, and as for me—well, I made it through somehow, I can't remember much—and Anette was waiting for us in a pastry shop—Well, after passing our final exams, we sat across from each other at a little round marble table eating ice cream. It was dreadfully hot, outside the street stretched glaring and dead, the waitress in the white lace apron could hardly stand on her feet, and our summer dresses stuck to the little red-lacquered chairs.

I remember the exact flavours of ice cream we were eating: Grete had raspberry, Ulla had coffee and Anette had chocolate with whipped cream. We were very solemn. It was practically a ritual act.

And suddenly we were discussing Doctor Alexander.

I felt a chill down to my fingertips. I thought of his brown face with the yellow-smoked teeth, his wind-tousled hair, and I remembered how he'd come to class once with an edelweiss in his buttonhole.

Ulla said:—In history, I had a question from a certain exam. Well, as you can imagine, I knew what to put down. I probably owe it to him that I passed with honours.

Anette said:—If only we'd kept him, even for just one class a week, I'd have finished up school, like you, I wouldn't have got into mischief.

Grete was silent. Red glints played in her long brown eyes, the golden down trembled at her nape, and she set a spoon full of raspberry ice back down on the glass dish.

Meanwhile I remembered my betrayal, and felt an ache, as insanely and unfathomably painful as the one I'd felt back then on the train after refusing Horky her kiss. I looked up from myself, away to the others.

Then we said goodbye on the blinding hot pavement outside the pastry shop. And it was a long time before we met again.

Oh yes, that's right, Ulla walked with me a little way down a long, narrow, very cool street. And suddenly she said:—Us four, why is it always us four? I really ought to be friends with Gerda Lange or Liselotte Meller. We have the same interests. But Grete and Anette kept getting in the way. Sometimes Anette almost disgusts me, and Grete is a well-bred young lady. And then there's you—you—

She stopped and stared at me with her blue ice-water eyes. Almost threateningly.

—You're the one who always wanted it that way. Really it's your fault.

I replied evasively:—We used to sit together all the time.

She gave me a nod and vanished around the corner.

Oh, how I feared she could vanish from my life now, just as Uncle Max had vanished that green-spuming summer afternoon, his black valise in his right hand. She could vanish, Anette could vanish, Grete—

It wasn't just fear. It was mortal fear.

Papa and Mama saw the state I was in and thought it was nervous strain. I was sent away, told to take a trip alone, alone for the first time ever. To the south, to the sea.

I was alone, I was terribly alone. In the hotels I stayed in, all the waiters had the same face, only the chambermaids were sad and tearful sometimes.

Yesterday Grete was tearful too. Grete! She came to ask me—oh God, I can't write it down, it's too ghastly—

I don't know if I should even go on writing at all . . . .

I answered her in a hoarse voice. A hoarse lie.

There I was, about to write about myself, myself alone, about how things were and how things happened as they did, but suddenly the days are too bright, as though there's no air between me and the sun, between me and the others.

The present has come so close. All you need to do is stretch out your hand, all you need is—

Oh God, anything but that!

I know all too well what it means to be betrayed when you're defenceless, carrying all life's perils, all death's perils inside a pregnant body. I know it well, even if he tries a thousand times to drag me off to healthy pleasures and stolen bliss.

Because he knows nothing, nothing, nothing about it! Hasn't the slightest notion. Not a notion!

But then, I know nothing about him either. Whenever I try to understand him, the incident with the sailor comes to mind. Actually, probably not a sailor, a beggar. But no matter.

So, they'd sent me on a trip, as I just mentioned, alone on a trip. I was supposed to rest up from all my studying.

One afternoon I went strolling along an Italian harbour. The sea was scalding blue and right across from the jaunty beach café, an enormous black warship lay at anchor. Men in grey smocks—they looked like convicts—were clambering about on it. In the café, the band was playing 'Celeste Aida'.

And the muzzles of the canons were pointed straight in that direction.

I was walking slowly, it was very hot and the music perturbed me, it smelled of tar and fish and salt, and suddenly I thought a dog was crawling across the street in front of me. I hated to look, hated to, because it was a man, a man, not a dog, a legless man on a tiny little cart, a man in a sailor's blouse, he looked at me, must have said something too, he looked up at me from below—There was something oozy about his gaze—and I gave him a few centesimi. Gingerly, trying not to touch him. He took them and cursed me.

And I walked on and the band played on and the man was gone, like a dog crossing the street, the street glowed dark yellow and I was alone, as alone as though I were wearing no clothes.

I shouldn't have given him those centesimi. I knew that. But he was as alien to me as though he'd rolled into the sea and lay hundreds of yards down, green and bloated on the seabed.

I should have touched him. I knew that. But I didn't sense it. Still don't sense it today. I never sense what a man is feeling.

Not even today.

After that incident I had a sudden yearning for Uncle Max. That's probably why I saw him that same evening on a poorly lit oil-fumy street, vanishing in front of me into the crowd. Of course it wasn't him, that's impossible, it was just Papa's shoulders, his haughty stride.

Some women were quarrelling, children shrieked, the air was like a dark bath, soon after that it must have started raining . . . .

No, I'm sure it wasn't Uncle Max. I don't understand why it still upsets me, I don't understand—

13 May. Last night Grete gave birth to a child. A son. His son.

I haven't written for three months now. Three months. It seems like it should be much longer. But the calendar says three months.

I spent all last night reading this, my life story; it is my life story, after all, however much it holds of Grete, Ulla and Anette. I calmed down, calm for the first time since that 13 May and since that night.

At first I'd resolved not to go on writing at all. All this scribbling's no help. If it were any help, none of this would ever have happened.

But yesterday when I was so alone, so terribly alone, at night, the window open, not even the stranger looming up behind the panes, the room vacant in fact, utterly vacant, no one inside, not a breath and not a soul, no pain and no yearning, in fact there was simply no one in my room—a burglar could have easily made off with everything—Then I got out the leather portfolio once more, that preposterous portfolio with the pressed roses and forget-me-nots and Herr Zaunegger's love letters, I'd piled everything together, these letters and these notes, these records, these proofs of my experiences . . . .

There's so much in there about Uncle Max, too. I should have burnt it all three months ago. But that would have hurt too much.

Now I want to start writing again. Maybe it'll help, and anyway, what harm can it do?

So, I'd stopped with the final exams, with that trip to the south, when a man, a sailor, maybe a beggar, dragged himself across the street like a dog, and that evening—

But then suddenly it's 13 May, Grete's son, yes, Grete's son, Axel's son.

I think I'll begin with this summer after all. When a thing's set down on paper, it's easier to get rid of. And I don't even quite recall what followed that solitary trip to Italy. Ulla was in her first year of medical school, with corpses to cut up and off-colour jokes from shirt-sleeved students, and Anette was living with a certain sculptress, no she wasn't, first it was the lingerie shop—

But I might as well write about all of that later. There's no hurry. Now the child is here, crying, kicking, growing, drinking milk from Grete's translucent breasts, acquiring eyebrows, a gaze and a face— There's no point in beating about the bush; I'm not afraid, after all, and actually it wasn't even me, that I know, that I can swear to, it wasn't me, it wasn't me who had that smothering cruel fear of losing him, why should I—however many thousand times the stranger floated in the mirror over the couch—

It's no one's fault but Grete's. I'd tell it to her face if she didn't already know. And Ulla's fault, with her infernal lack of scruples, her principles of free and easy camaraderie, and Anette's, with her squinty eyes and her pea-green silk chemises.

The stranger is the only innocent party. Because she's the only one who's not in love with Axel.

Come to think of it, if I write down the whole story right here, it'll show who it was, everything will be cleared up, set straight, set right—just a few pages more, and I'll calmly write about myself, about my life, my plans and my goals, I'll write more about Papa and Mama, the university, the lectures, my bout of appendicitis the second year, the library and Herr Zaunegger.

God, if only it weren't so boring!

On 13 May, at 7.30 in the evening—

Well, naturally it's all Grete's fault. What person these days gets the vulgar notion of giving birth at home—!

That's not the done thing, that's indecent, Ulla says. She, Ulla, would naturally go to a clinic with delivery wards and an operating room and nurses in white, and Anette might give birth under a railway bridge, in a roadside ditch if that's how it happened to turn out, but certainly not in her own bed, right next to the parlour, and all just for the beauty of the thing.

Yes, the beauty!

On the evening of 13 May I phoned Grete's house. I can't remember why, it was probably about something completely superfluous. I phoned and asked to speak to Herr Professor—I was still calling him Herr Professor then—and heard an unfamiliar agitated voice.

Later I realized that it must have been Ulla.

So it was happening now! I gazed out at the library's high, arched windows, the distant towers of the city swimming in sulphur-yellow haze, golden laburnum cascading over the parks' cast-iron grilles—and I saw Grete, delicate and untouchable, at the school desk in front of me, a gentle breath of air stirring her nape's golden down, she was dressed in British cloth, looked after by a strong handsome father, and all for this, to lie pain-bloated, groaning unsouled to heave a child, a stupid child, a red bundle of human flesh into the world.

Of course I went to see Grete. Why did I go to her, really? The streetcars rang their bells in alarm. A lorry nearly ran over me. No, Uncle Max's hairy hands should never have been allowed to touch Grete.

All the streets opened up. People, dogs, poured out of the houses, women leaned out all the windows. Grete, Grete, for God's sake, Grete!

I swear, I swear it by all I hold sacred—but what do I hold sacred any more?—well anyway I swear: when I went to see Grete that evening, I was thinking only of her, of her alone.

Who knows, it might have been better if I'd thought of her less.

But when I stepped inside the house, that cool, self-assured villa with the close-shaven little front yard, I sensed something utterly alien, something unconnected to Grete. Something hostile.

A person passed me carrying white linens, Ulla was wearing a white coat, a woman in a huge white apron gave orders, white ether filtered through the dense white walls, and white groans—I saw Grete's father nearly aswim in the white fog, he gave me his hand. I felt as though my legs were being sawed off at the knees—Grete's mother—a distant graveyard filled with tulips and hyacinths—Now the daughter, the girl, the delicate golden girl was lying ill and yammering in a strange bed—A groaning, a wailing, a bellowing—

Grete was bellowing!

At that I must have lost my senses. Doors slammed. The entire house, the sensible walls with the well-chosen pictures, the tall tiled heating stoves, were webbed by trembling red arteries. I clapped my hands over my ears, dashed down a hall, ran into something bony, stared into a face pale with horror, Axel—But I ran past him out onto the street where the sudden darkness stopped my ears, ran past a girl in high-heeled shoes.

That was cowardly, of course it was cowardly, but if I'd stayed in that house—I would have bellowed too.

So I was alone in my own four walls, running back and forth, at one point I even tore the mirror from the wall, looking for the stranger—and before me I saw a dead, pain-twisted face such as I'd never seen before, lips gaping in a torment that might have been a smile. But not a human smile.

Then I lapsed into a stifling sleep.

The next day Ulla came to the library to tell me that Grete had given birth to a son.

I nodded, that was all. I noticed huge circles under Ulla's eyes. She had assisted with the birth.—It wasn't an easy birth, but a normal one, she said. I glanced at her hands. She still had those porcelain-white clever wrists, but her fingers were long and coarse and red. Working hands.

That, in fact, was why she had such wonderfully well-kept skin, a skin that made her hard features look soft and supple. Cream and powder.

—Yes, yes, I said, I'll drop by this evening or tomorrow.

I went home, set down a certain entry in my notes: 13.5. Last night Grete gave birth to a son. And after that I couldn't write for three months.

Because then it happened, the awful thing, the crime. Really a crime? Can what's a matter of course be a crime?

And above all: Was it me? If someone could come and prove it, maybe the stranger, if the stranger could prove to me that I'd done it, I, the one Papa and Mama kept forgetting in the corner as a child, I, the one who loved Uncle Max, the one who betrayed Horky, that time when—

Oh God, now everything's blurring again. And it just occurred to me that today I'm supposed to remind him about the letter to the American university. How could I forget something that important!

But back to that night. All this is just evading the issue. It shall be set down black on white. And then I'll know that I, I am a nasty person, a vampire, a thief, perhaps even a murderess soon.

Well, if that's how it is, at least I want to know it for myself.

Two days after 13 May, I finally visited Grete. I hadn't seen the baby yet. It was quite late, around 8. But after all, I've got my work, I've got to be at the library, I can't just run around during working hours visiting women in childbed.

The white villa was as silent, as dead as a place is only after a hideous racket. A mild quiet rain was coming down.

A girl in a white nurse's pinafore sternly raised a finger to her lips. Grete was sleeping. The girl pointed to a door. I went in. It was Axel's study.

Good Lord, I'd known Axel a long time by that point. I'd always fancied him, of course, after all I had let him kiss me, he was strong, blond, superior and often a touch indifferent.

Today, though, today he seemed utterly changed. He was sitting all alone in his big club chair, he was pale, maybe ill, he was sad and he was hungry.

Yes, hungry, that was it. When he looked at me with his little, pale, famished eyes, an unhappy little boy—the first thing I did was head for the kitchen. The maids were nowhere to be seen. Oh, it's a splendid kitchen, spick and span with blue stripes, and right away I found everything we needed, hard-cooked eggs and a bit of salad. Butter and cheese and a plate full of cherries. He was delighted. Especially about the cherries. We spat the stones onto a plate.

Maybe everything would have turned out differently if he hadn't mentioned Ulla. How capable she was, what a soothing effect she had in all the hubbub yesterday—and—His pale restless eyes gazed at me, past me, through me, out the window, and I was seized by the senseless, foolish, cruel, wrenching fear of losing him.

Because if he got up right now and went away, away from me, he'd go looking for Ulla in her quiet cool room at the clinic, unless he stopped on the street to escort Anette, oh, fiddlesticks, Anette, some Anette or other.

His eyes were so hungry. And suddenly through the sleep-dead stillness of the house there came a wretched puling as of a tiny naked animal.

I can't, I can't write down what happened. No one would believe me, not a soul, and the worst thing is, I don't believe myself.

All I know is, suddenly everything was changed, the chair next to me, the desk with the sensible glass lamp. As though draped in white cloths, silent sheets. There was a smell of severed white hyacinths, I was terribly sad and I was afraid. But I saw that Axel was hungry, and I smiled and lowered my head, delicate and gentle I lowered my head and rosy down seemed to curl on my nape.

Deep blue Riviera air poured through the window. Next to me on the chair lay a white, a flowing-white silk shirt. It appalled me that he had a beard, he was beautifully shaved, but he had a beard all the same, and when he kissed me on the mouth, I wanted to cry out: Father, father!

But I didn't, because the room was filled with incense, candles burning, countless candles, alien words, murmurs, red wine and champagne glasses—Father, father!

Oh I suffered agonies. As though something unspeakably precious were being given away, squandered and obliterated.

Women like Grete shouldn't get married. They should take the veil, have their likenesses chiselled as heavenly virgins and set in white stone on flickering altars.

I wrote that two days ago. Afterwards I was so tired that I fell into bed still holding the pencil. When I read it the next evening, it seemed vile and dishonest. Today I was reluctant to look at it again. But it isn't dishonest at all.

It's true. That wedding night is true, when he took me like a delicate, precious girl, an utter, utter stranger. My god, why won't anyone believe me when I say it smelled of hyacinths, and a strange blue breeze swam with stars.

It's also true, of course—or maybe not?—that for one entire spring I, a librarian with a pension fund, etc. etc., and my colleague, Head Librarian Max Zaunegger had—what do you call it—relations. Relations—what a ghastly expression, by the way.

I'll write about that too, naturally, that goes without saying. Hopefully I won't doze off over my papers.

And it's also true, of course, that in the shivering dawn I woke up fully dressed on a strange, stained couch. Fully dressed—oh, that was ugly! As Ulla says, we women always need there to be some beauty in it. She even says: We poor women always need there to be some beauty in it. We poor women?

Grete isn't poor. I mean, it's absurd even to think such a thing. And Grete wasn't poor when she sat gentle and sweet and near and infinitely remote in front of me at school, she wasn't even poor when her dear kind mother died and she crossed the graveyard threshold with her father, because she always knew exactly how lovely she was, how people yearned to possess her. Oh that yearning! Doctor Alexander exuded that yearning when he walked into the classroom and called on Grete even though he knew she wasn't there. All along Grete moved in a way that was like bathing, as though immersing herself in the feelings of the others, of the men. That was how it had always been. But it was worst or best of all in Gera, Gera or Giessen or Göttingen, what was it called again, some little university town. Her father had been transferred there just after we finished school, and Grete went along with him to—well, let's say to G.

G.—there was that girl G. E. too. But that's neither here nor there.

Several weeks after moving Grete sent me a postcard from G. Grete was altogether one for writing postcards, she still is, there was one just yesterday with a green forest on it: Now we're coming back for good at the end of the week. The child is well. I am fine.

For good! Yes indeed, Fräulein Librarian, there's nothing to be done. You can't go on forever lying in bed, no, in someone else's conjugal bed, smiling her smile, sharing her joys, her shudders, but always smiling, smiling through it all, and having physics experiments explained to you without understanding a word.

So, Grete sent me a postcard from G., as I mentioned, that was several years ago, I was in my first semester of history and that postcard was—well like any postcard really. A street with trees, actually a great many trees, and a pointed tower floating somewhere in the sky.

Around the corner from that main street, which even had a streetcar jingling along, stood the professor's house. It wasn't a large house with a large garden, but still it was a pale palace with tall windows, and the sleek lawn with its beeches was a park.

It smelled of rotting leaves and split-open horse chestnuts when Grete and her father moved in. She stood there hatless in her travelling coat in the October sun and gave orders for unpacking the crates. The hair curled at her nape, her hoarse voice was soft, but the moving men listened to her all the same. A bunch of students passed behind the picket fence, on the second floor the professor flung open a window, his silver head leaned out, and maidservants and neighbour ladies peeked over all the hedges.

That evening a fire blazed in the grand fireplace. The table was laid with the silver that still bore Grete's mother's monogram.

It was a laid-out life in a sheltered town among well-secured people. A life pieced together like a gentle jigsaw puzzle.

My life was never laid-out, sheltered, secure. Not even when Papa was a wealthy banker and Mama took Bea to society affairs. Because of Horky, with her coarse hands, who tromped around our high-class kitchen as if it were a Czech stable, and Uncle Max, who was liable to vanish at any time, maybe to America, maybe to India, maybe just to some stranger's flat. And then there was Ulla with her leather couch in her father's operating room (I'm convinced she has a sand-coloured duvet in her room at the hospital) and Anette with her impudent fingers and that red rayon curtain in the hair salon—not to mention the market women, the girls at the street corners, the blue-pinafored women in the hospitals.

For three months I hadn't thought about any of that. For three months I was secure and reassured. For three months I knew I had only to smile, smile with broad translucent teeth, and Axel would emerge from the next room as though pulled by silver wires.

But yesterday I broke a teacup, one of the expensive, petal-thin ones with the cobalt rims. Axel was quite put out. And in the mirror, distraught and wild-eyed, the stranger appeared.

It was the first time that the stranger had appeared in one of Grete's mirrors. Grete's coming back at the end of the week.

Today Herr Zaunegger brought me flowers. For the first time since last spring. Chrysanthemums that look like yellow heads of cabbage.

Oh the flowers in G.! G. is a town of gardens, really. Roses outside every house, beds of roses outside the university, roses in all the vases, roses downstairs in the hall in an opalescent glass, roses in June, warmth-giving, resplendent, glowing and glowing, roses in a fog-white November behind picket fences covered in red woodbine.

Naturally everyone gave Grete roses, the students she danced with light and cool at the great balls, foreign scholars who visited her father, little girls with crushes on her. The whole town knew her, at the grocer and Frau Schultze's hair salon conversation revolved around the town's new belle.

One day a man would come, a lecturer or professor, a man still young and strong, with broad shoulders and a good salary, to take her with him to a silent house, the kitchen white with blue stripes, well-chosen pictures, club chairs, shaded lamps and a sensible nurse. And then a bit of pain. Dread and aversion, then yearning again when the evenings grew long, the room empty . . . .

Of all Grete's beaux—beau is a chambermaid word, says Ulla—of all her boyfriends, then—no, boyfriends are what Anette has, and they pay for her champagne and fluffy furs—well then, let's say of all the men who nosed around the professor's villa, curious yet cautious, the one Grete liked best was the private lecturer with the high forehead, the sick wife and all the small children. He was in a very particular field, Chinese philosophy or Persian or something equally outlandish, and he was a refined person, reticent and soulful. There was no danger of clutching hands and hot breath, of sudden proposals; he was married, after all. His home smelled of wet diapers and red flannels, the children pilfered sugar from the coffee-table, the maidservant raced through the rooms in a suspiciously clean apron and the lady of the house sat in an armchair wrapped in a woollen shawl, having just got out of bed in Fräulein Gretchen's honour—she called her Gretchen, she'd learnt that from her husband. Her eyes drooped, her breasts drooped and when she wasn't talking, her chin drooped.

Of course it was awkward for Grete that they turned the household upside-down just for her, that they fetched cake from the pastry shop and cigarettes from the cafe across the way, that the maidservant was fired that evening because the milk had boiled over, and the children were sent to bed with smacks and a scolding. She even felt a bit sorry for the man when he escorted her home through streets lined with well-kept villas, she felt like taking him with her to lay him down in a quiet room and stroke his brow. His neckties were always so frayed at the edges.

I can't stand how, now that it's cold, Axel's started wearing woollen undershirts. He did that even in the summer when it rained.

Actually, the private lecturer reminded Grete of that assistant who'd kissed her on the nape one Sunday morning. It was a slippery kiss, very disagreeable, and then she never saw him again. What a pity!

This time she was going to be more careful. Why cause people pain? No, Grete was a good person, she didn't want to hurt anyone. And she gave the private lecturer in the outlandish field the gift of long afternoons spent with his sick wife, his many too many children.

And she never would have learnt that in those gentle hours she'd been hated like a snake in the grass, that in the nights that followed, nights she never imagined, for what did we know of marriage, ah Grete, what did we know of marriage, maybe something of love, but nothing of marriage—that in those nights she was the cause of venomous rows. She never would learnt if it hadn't been for the drama with that boy.

He was a stupid boy, really. It's horrid to say that about a dead person, especially in this particular case. And it wasn't even love, I'm sure it was vanity. But who knows after the fact? At any rate, it wasn't good for Grete's reputation, people judged her unfairly, and the lecturer's proposal on top of it all, a marriage proposal from a married man! Not to mention the Italian count.

Then Axel showed up to save her and instantly all was well. Axel!

I can't help remembering a crazy day I had this summer. First there was unpleasantness at the library, and in the streetcar it was so hot that you stuck to the seat, a thin salty stripe of sweat ran down the conductor's uniform, the ticket he gave me was damp, the wall across the way was blindingly bright, something huge and black ran into us, a monster, crashing and splintering—

No, I wasn't hurt, just a cut on my left index finger, women screaming, the whistles of the ambulance brigade—

I walked and walked, I wasn't hurt, but I felt as though Grete were lying mangled under the wreckage of the automobile that had collided with us.

Yet as I went up the stairs Axel came down to meet me, he led me into his cellar-cool study, bandaged my hand, brought me lemonade, and everything was good and solid and safe. He slipped the pillow from his bed under my neck, and there I lay, and I was utterly calm.

But I meant to tell about the boy. His name was Hans Jürgen and he had a duelling scar across his cheek. Which, incidentally, they all did in G. And his mother was the widow of a privy councillor, a rector. She set the fashion in town, held an intellectual salon, talked a lot about art, had a great shock of false white hair and took Grete under her wing. That motherless young girl!

And Hans Jürgen fell in love with Grete, which was perfectly natural. He fell in love a bit more than the others, but Grete couldn't know that, really she couldn't. He had a rosy childish face with blurry eyes, a pretty face, really too pretty for a boy. And because he was so pretty and delicate, he became the best boxer, he went on the wildest car rides. Oh, what a fool he was. And Grete liked him well enough. No one can fault her for that. No one can fault her at all for the way men fell in love with her. Maybe she should have run after them like the other girls. Then of course she'd have been rid of the lot. If she'd given the private lecturer just one look, sideways like—he'd have gone back to his wife that very same evening. But she didn't do that. Ever.

And that's why they all wanted to possess her.

Then came that absurd business with the wager. No, the privy chancellor's widow never found out about it, and she mustn't ever find out. She thinks it was sheer passion on the part of a deluded young man, and of course it was, but unfortunately with that wager on top of things.

It was Midsummer's night, which was celebrated in G. with a grand ball and processions and bonfires on the hills. The students marched to the outskirts of town and descended on all the inns, the liquor flowed too—but that's the last thing the privy councillor's widow should ever be told about. Since that day she's been in mourning, with a little black bonnet on her shock of white hair.

In G. all the roses were spreading their fragrance. Naturally that was intoxicating too. All around on the rolling hills the bonfires burned, guitars were strummed, girls' voices, white frocks, sweet white frocks.

Grete was never lovelier than she was that night. Her eyes blazed, her mouth swelled, a bit too big, a bit too red—

No, I mustn't write that. That's a betrayal. No one must know. No one. Women like Grete don't speak, they never speak, even if you tear their hearts out.

I can't help it, there was a man at that ball, a stranger, tall and dark and supple, an Italian, a count, his mouth a fine fixed line, brownish cheeks.

He danced as no man had ever danced with Grete, he danced like a supple southern animal.

Axel wasn't there, off on a trip that day.

But the Italian pulled Grete into a corner behind garlands of paper roses, he bent her head back, or maybe they were still dancing, and he kissed her—

It was only a kiss, but no one must ever hear about it, for the narrow line of his lips parted, gentle, delicate, slightly rotten petals, along with the grip of brutal fingers.

Of course she pushed him off, with Grete that goes without saying—but not right away.

Because Grete won't say it and Grete doesn't want it and Grete won't admit it and Grete doesn't know it, doesn't guess that she loved that man. That he was the only one she let kiss her on the mouth.

That night some of the guests' valuables went missing, and the next day the Italian count had vanished. He turned out to be a taxi dancer from one of the surrounding spa towns, not a count, maybe not even Italian.

He was never caught. Thank goodness for that!

Is it permissible to write that? Is it permissible to put a thing like that in writing? Women like Grete suffocate on their unlived life and smile the whole time.

I hate it when Axel kisses me on the mouth, but I smile too. With Herr Zaunegger, I simply put my foot down.

Hans Jürgen, that foolish boy, didn't want to kiss Grete on the mouth. He wanted a much simpler thing. He wanted to spirit her away in his new Chrysler and take her up the hill where he and his friends had the town's biggest bonfire, of course theirs was the biggest, and at the stroke of midnight.

He did it on a wager, the private lecturer would never have got wind of it otherwise, and Hans Jürgen's breath smelled of wine when he suddenly invited Grete, right in the middle of the ball, to come see his new Chrysler, and Grete would have, too, but suddenly the private lecturer stepped between them and lost his temper. Grete was so lovely, so tremulously lovely that night, and Hans Jürgen got rude, very rude, and the private lecturer slapped him in the face and Hans Jürgen was about to lunge, but Grete intervened, suddenly thinking of that sick wife and all those children.

Hans Jürgen got into his Chrysler and raced up to the bonfire on the hill, the biggest and grandest bonfire of all, 90 km/h, and when he stopped, he put a bullet through his head.

The people of G. are talking about it to this day. Hans Jürgen was buried with full honours. They called the whole thing an affair of honour. Honour?

Ulla says honour's a bourgeois invention. Axel has honour too, he'd never, ever put up with a slap in the face. When he dies, they'll print his name in the papers, just like now it's printed at all the congresses. Axel can be relied on. Recently when I didn't send the girl to pay the phone bill on time, he got seriously angry.

He loves order in all things. It was awfully decent of him to ask for Grete's hand after that ill-starred Midsummer night. Once she was his fiancée, no one dared cast aspersions on her.

The privy chancellor's old widow even wrote her a lovely, touching letter. Grete showed it to no one, really she didn't, but the whole town was talking about it.

The whole town was talking about the private lecturer's proposal too. It's incredible, the way things get around in a small town like that.

The unfortunate fellow suddenly showed up hat one rainy morning in a top hat—honest to God, he was wearing a top hat, when Grete saw him, she thought there was a funeral—and asked for Grete's hand. Grete was wearing a dark-blue dress and stared at him with damp and horrified eyes. Then she looked out the window. All of a sudden the lawn was so small, brown moisture dripped from the beeches. It was a simple house she lived in, really, an ordinary villa, the type you find in every German university town. Through the park—but it wasn't a park—though the garden, a gaunt woman walked with her head down, strung up a clothesline, hung diapers, red flannels, she bent over, gold down on her wrinkled nape. That wasn't her, no, no, surely that wasn't her.

Grete shook her head. The private lecturer fell to his knees. How preposterous! One more thing that could happen only in a small town. He spoke of his wife, of two separate beds, of curses and vows, of the sick woman's hatred of the lovely, healthy girl, of late-night scenes, venomous squabbles—all of it, all because of his love for her.

One time that spring when we went to the mountains every weekend Herr Zaunegger also accused me of the horridest things because—well, I've forgotten why. It must have been someone in the train or a waiting room or the overcrowded bus. He had golden glasses and a mountain tan and reminded me of Doctor Alexander, or maybe Axel—I don't remember whether I spoke to him. Maybe that was the reason. At any rate, that night Herr Zaunegger sat up in his bed, extremely upset. It was a grey bed, grey sheets and a stifling red quilt, one washbasin held a bit of grey water with soap scum—

It was awful. Grete didn't know what to do. Luckily her father walked in the door and put an end to the scene. Down below, the garden looked dark and unkempt like the garden of an abandoned signal-keeper's house.

And how grand it was the next day when Axel appeared blond and cheerful downstairs in the hall. The sun darted through rainclouds, he wasn't wearing a top hat, oh, no, he came in his lab coat, and with a teeny little ink spot on his middle finger.

His fountain pen's being repaired. I mustn't forget to pick it up tomorrow. Grete's coming on Thursday. Thursday—that's two days from now. Grete and the nurse and the child.

And Axel spoke to Grete's father, spoke of the wedding as lightly and casually as of a summer holiday. Towards evening he strolled with her across the lawn in front of the house, the villa, the palace, and the lawn stretched wide, sloping up soft and velvet. The beeches glowed in the setting sun, daisies and golden windows—Then Axel put his arm around me and everything turned soft and white, the flowing shirt, candles suffused with incense, champagne bubbles, blossoms and veils, but the air was blue, deep-blue Riviera air.

He shouldn't have kissed me on the mouth. His lips tasted of blood.

Yes, I know, you'd need to kiss him the way Ulla kisses, the way women kiss who've learnt how—even kissing can be learnt. Ulla's learnt a lot, she's learnt everything, she discusses his experiments with him, sometimes even wrinkling her nose. That nose always has a bit too much powder. As a child, Ulla would get freckles in the summer.

I say, that Herr Zaunegger really has no shame. What's he after with those yellow cabbages of his? I can't live without Axel. I can't. Are they trying to lop off my legs? How should I—even cross the street—without him? . . . .

Ulla's meeting him at the physics department again. I daresay they're even on first-name terms.

I don't want to live without him. The fountain pen still isn't fixed yet. Who will go get his fountain pen?

Tomorrow Grete's coming.

Every time things go utterly insane and intolerable, the stranger appears. No, I don't like that stranger, I couldn't stand her even back the first time I saw her in the mirror on the train. My sister Bea was eating bread with yellow cheese and I had just betrayed Horky . . .

Now I've betrayed Grete.

But what does the stranger care? Why does she have to act so offended? Come to think of it, what's she doing sitting beside me in the streetcar? Till now she was always in mirrors and windows, probably didn't even exist, a spectre, a dream, fantasy, hysteria—But today, no doubt about it, today she sat beside me in the streetcar, holding a dog-eared book, weary and sad.

I felt sorry for her. And that is what's so dreadful, so intolerable. Where will it end? I mustn't feel sorry for her, for the stranger. Because there's no air and no light between her and me. I can't go to her.

Grete has arrived. The little boy has a touch of the stomach flu. My goodness, I'm sure that's something all children get. But Axel's very worried, he's phoning all the doctors.

For me it's a good thing. Now at least there's an end to it all. Of course I can live without Axel. What was I to him! At most a surrogate.

Recently he remarked, awfully surprised:—You've got brown hair. Really, you'd think he could have noticed that before. And in fact he's not so awfully clever. Ulla says he's idiotic when talk turns to politics.

Oh Ulla, Ulla! If only it weren't for Ulla! When I think of her, and I think of her a lot these days, I'm stricken by that insane, senseless, wrenching fear of losing him. It's as though I were being expelled from a quiet safe room, perhaps a white kitchen with blue stripes.

Ulla mustn't, she simply mustn't. Ulla's cheeky with him, she doesn't respect him. You don't just steal a man like Axel from his wife, his beautiful and beloved wife, simply because he's broad-shouldered and wiry and has a sweet boyish laugh, and because you're impatient and hopelessly in love with a chief physician.

No, I won't put up with it. Even if I'm just a librarian with Herr Zaunegger as my beau, even if I read dog-eared books on the streetcar, even if I'm such a bore and write such trivial stuff that I have to fill page after page evening after evening to reassure myself that it's really me who's living this life—

I won't put up with it. And I'll find a way to stop it.

Of course I can't stop a thing. I have no say at all. I haven't seen Axel for a week now. Meanwhile I can tell that autumn has come, withered leaves in the park, a rustling underfoot, damp roofs, the lights on warm evenings burning intrusively.

Wasn't there any summer, blue waves, ripening grainfields in humid haze? What's wrong with me? I'm shivering? Who—robbed—me—of—my—summer? . . . .

Today Axel came to see me in the library. He knows what's proper. He was very friendly. Very kind. Invited me to lunch. He spent five minutes standing there with me. Five minutes isn't a long time. I gazed at the big clock between the crowded bookshelves. Five minutes isn't a long time. He was very kind, very friendly. For those brief five minutes I bored him dreadfully.

A thing like that mustn't be mentioned, a thing like that mustn't be put into words. Grete wouldn't even have told it to her mother. She's very pale, much too thin, with huge rings under her eyes.

And she's afraid of the night. The baby's hungry, she doesn't have enough milk—And Axel—I'd love to bring him another plate of cherries. He wouldn't even have to spit the pits on a plate with me. He has such little famished eyes.

Oh, it's awful, it's appalling, it's more than I can bear. Of course, I can't stop a thing, but I can't just put up with it, before my very eyes, at the very same table—Can you call that love, much less marriage?

I shouldn't have gone to that luncheon, at first I didn't want to, I'd already promised to go to the Natural History Museum with Herr Zaunegger Sunday morning, when suddenly I felt it was the proper thing to do.

How stupid of me! Bea also felt it was the proper thing to marry that *Herr von* .... Supposedly the eldest son's a bit queer in the head. What do I care what's proper? Am I Bea?

I went to that damned lunch. It was raining. The clean-shaved front yard was aswim in grey water. The nursery was distinctly overheated. And Ulla's perfume was too strong. That's no way to enter a home with an infant and a nursing mother. She has a fabulous complexion. It can't be makeup. Maybe facial massage and that sort of thing.

Axel's mad for her, simply mad. And all because she wants it. Because every movement of her porcelain wrists, every slantwise look is calculated. Her mouth is crimson red. But he won't let Grete paint her pale tired lips. When Ulla refuses soup, he's enthused, when she smokes blue rings, he's entranced. He lays his arm around the back of her chair as though it were her shoulders, tender and cautious.

No, no, no! I'll kill her, I'll murder her. I can't stand to watch. The next time I'll slam my hand down on the table so hard the glasses shatter. By God, I don't have to stand for being torn in two, dismembered and chopped up alive—

Who's that laughing? I'm sure someone was laughing. Ulla? Nonsense, where is Ulla? But it was Ulla's voice. A bit too bright, like cracked porcelain. The lamp's reflected in the window. The stranger, the stranger, where on earth is she? Next to the lamp there's just a pair of cold eyes, glacier-clear, icy eyes, greedy eyes and a bold, laughing mouth—Don't look, no, don't and for God's sake, don't laugh!

Trying again. I'm writing in the library. At my official desk. No one's laughing here. Herr Zaunegger has a new inkstand and exudes furious severity. Because of Sunday, of course.

Rereading what I wrote yesterday, it seems a bit over the top. This sober white-painted room with the prim rainy light is the best place to come to reason.

Ulla says libraries are deathly dull. Well, the hospital can't be much fun either.

But back to last night's laughter. I was so startled that I dropped everything, dove into bed and pulled the covers over my head.

How stupid! After all, I had every reason to laugh. Didn't I? Isn't it laughable that I should be jealous, I of all people? Jealous of Ulla? As though I had any right. Me—with a right to Axel. A laughable impertinence!

Grete—yes, Grete's a different matter. But Grete will never say so, just bites her bloodless lips, suffocating.

What will they blame it on when Grete dies? Pneumonia, a weak heart? When her mother was carried to her grave, the cemetery was a beaming mass of tulips and hyacinths. Grete leaned on her handsome father's arm. But I saw her ill and parched with fever in a strange bed. A little girl. A proud little girl.

Oh God, I can't let anything happen to her. Her mother was crippled. I won't stand for it. I'll go to her. I'll speak to her.

But is it possible to speak to Grete? When she smiles with broad translucent teeth, she's the lovely child again with golden down on her nape, sitting next to Anette on the bench in front of me, far beyond reach.

Then I'll try Ulla. Ulla's always one for openness and having things out. And Ulla's clever, a bit too clever, but certainly not wicked.

I'll go see her at the hospital today. There's something to be said for sitting in a public library at broad noon and writing your—your life story. Is it really my life story?

So. Now I'm back sitting at my desk, by my lamp. The lampshade's not exactly presentable, the walls are covered in soot. I'll have them painted this spring, this time not grey but dull yellow, sand-yellow, and no pictures.

Really I should be writing about more important things. But I'm so calm, so incredibly calm. Maybe the whole affair with Axel isn't such a burning issue after all. All men are like that. Most of them are. Grete won't take it too hard.

My mirror's sprung a crack. That's why I don't like to look in it. But that's no good, your hair never lies straight unless you keep brushing it. There's something soothing about smooth hair that stays put.

I think I'll go to bed. I'm exhausted. Tomorrow I can write about my visit to Ulla at the hospital. I won't see Axel again. Maybe never again. Good night.

A week later. A whole week and maybe two hours. For a week I haven't written, probably never would have written again if Axel hadn't—

It's all because he's such a conventional person. Even when life's no longer the least bit conventional, when it's deranged, distorted and crazy—yes, crazy.

So, he dropped by this evening—I want to say right off that a lot of things have changed here the past week. The lampshade is new, not especially nice, but nice enough that you don't even notice there's a lamp on the table now, and a thick, woolly soft green blanket is laid on the couch.

Good lord, it gets on my nerves, the way I keep changing the subject—And if Axel came to visit, what of it. Why part on bad terms after three months of—

Oh, fiddlesticks, Axel was very sweet and very polite, told me stories from work, kissed the tips of my fingers when he left.

Grete's sick, by the way. She's having great trouble weaning the baby—Actually, Grete is sick quite a lot.

There's no crack in the mirror any more. New glass. But I can't look in it. Though my hair's hanging into my eyes and I'm sure I've got those corkscrew curls again. I'm afraid—

What am I afraid of this time? I ought to be locked away in a hospital—Yes, a hospital. Not everyone in a hospital has to be a doctor, there are patients there too. Patients in white beds in long white wards at the end of long white halls, and down those halls the chief physician comes trailing a long procession of assistants—Hush, hush, the chief physician's coming.

Oh that hush! I remember how agitated I was before going to see Ulla. I hadn't had lunch, I took a cab and left three books (library books!) behind on the seat. I stumbled on Ulla's name when I told it to the porter at the garden gate. The sky was cold and green. Long red clouds drifted above the huge white boxy buildings. In hospital gardens the grass is sparse, the trees bare and gaunt, and sickly—

But that doesn't matter a bit once you're walking down the corridors, those wonderful white gentle corridors. No matter what happens, a white-dressed girl brings a bucket of disinfectant and washes it away. The elevators function impeccably. Though a glass door you peek into a ward filled with pale women in quiet white beds. Oh no, they've no cause for agitation, all's going fine and all's in order, there's a big white clock in each ward, and everything arrives according to that clock, meals, fevers, agonies, death, and now and then the chief physician.

I saw him. By chance. At first I couldn't find Ulla's room, the corridors are so long, they all look alike, and suddenly he was walking towards me.

He doesn't really have a face, but he has a white coat and gentle colourless eyes. A pale bald crown and colourless bony hands. The other doctors hung back a bit behind him. Because he has a limp. Yes, a limp.

A nurse pulled me aside, I was standing rooted to the spot, three more steps and he would have walked into me. I don't remember how I got to Ulla's room after that.

Ulla was sitting at an immaculately set table drinking tea, tea with nothing in it, tea with no sugar. Next to the tea was a plate full of apples. No pictures on the walls, no curtains at the windows. But opulent little bottles glittered on the dressing table. And of course, Ulla was wearing that white coat.

She gave me her hand:—What's ailing you?

Yes, what was ailing me? I sank down onto the smooth yellowish linen cushions of her chaise-longue and she took my pulse and gave me a few drops of something in a glass of water.

Of course now I couldn't mention Grete and the whole silly business with Axel.

—Does this happen to you often?—Almost every day. And it's always worst when I smell meat broth. Then it's almost too much to stand.

Ulla frowned and said as matter-of-factly as a book:—Are you worried that you might having a baby?

The girl G. E.! Why, oh why had I said the same thing the girl G. E. said? And Ulla went on talking as calmly and gently as you talk to, well, a patient. I pretended to listen, thinking instead of the black leather couch in the operating room, she turned on the shadeless bulb, I closed my eyes, blinded, on her bed lay a sand-coloured duvet.

Where was Hermann, her friend, her comrade? A brown mop of hair, olives, caustically salty, meltingly oily olives. He had a shy, stand-offish way of offering his hand, but when you clasped it, you were honoured and elevated.

The chief physician must have been coming back down the hall now. Limping.

Ulla gave me a powder, too. Was that what made me so tired and calm that I had no idea what to write that evening and was in bed by 9.30 reading the paper?

And everything would have been fine and orderly and I wouldn't even think about Grete any more. What's it to me if she's having trouble weaning the baby, if Axel loves her enough, if the kitchen with the blue stripes is tidy, she's got her child—

By the way, it's odd that Ulla should ask me such a thing right off the bat. And a thing like that's never out of the question. It's just that you don't think about it.

That girl G. E. Oh God!

Right, what was I trying to say, everything would have been fine if only Axel hadn't shown up at my door. He looked around, said:— You've got a nice place here (as if anyone ever thought my room was nice), and later on he kissed my hand, very carefully, just the fingertips, and I held them out to him like a woman who's thinking of someone else entirely. And that's why he'll come back.

Now Ulla, she'd never have cared the least bit for Herr Zaunegger. In fact, she'd arch her eyebrows if he requested the pleasure of taking her to a cafe. You see, she arches her brows sometimes when something doesn't sit right with her, it's more devastating than obscenities from anyone else. And then that ice-water stare! Utterly impossible!

But that Zaunegger really is an impossible person. I'm convinced he's got excess white blood cells and endocrine problems. Plus a moustache like a worn-out children's toothbrush.

And if it weren't for Fräulein Marschall at the desk next to mine with her questioning googly eyes, if she weren't always sharpening his pencils before he arrives in the morning and offering him her thermos tea at 10 in the morning, I never would have dreamt any woman in the world could ever like him. But she loves him. She lies in wait for him. She has a plush coat that's supposed to look like fur. And knitted gloves. She wants to marry him.

No, you don't grab a man like Herr Zaunegger for the fun of it. The only reason Fräulein Marschall wants him is that she's a foolish old maid who doesn't even know what a man is.

I was his first proper relationship, by the way. Otherwise all he had was—

That swine used an expression I won't sully this paper with. Naturally Herr Head Librarian can buy himself women, a woman on every street corner—

The next thing you know, we'll be buying ourselves men! Faugh!

Axel has a car now. Really, he's needed one for ages, he lives so far away from the physics institute, but he's thrifty, God knows why he waited so long.

And he looks good, damned good as a chauffeur. He wears a leather jacket now, fortunately not too brand-new looking, and shirts with soft collars. Today he picked me up from home in his car. He smelled ever so slightly of petrol. If only I don't fall in love with him! He's got hands like a mechanic.

If I do the arithmetic right, maybe I can buy a fur on an instalment plan, a pale-grey one that caresses your whole body.

So, just now Anette came breezing in. She was in St Moritz and now she has an engagement at the Chat Noir, we've all got to come for the opening night. Grete, Ulla, Axel too, of course. Yesterday her mother came to bring me the ticket.

I don't actually believe that Anette's on the Riviera, all the time, in St Moritz or anywhere else posh. No. Everything she wears may be new, smooth and glossy, but it looks as if she bought it in St Pölten. Though maybe in the nicest shop. Her stockings are washable silk.

When she showed up at the library to see me yesterday, Herr Zaunegger practically flew into a rage. He was dying to throw her out, though in the evening, when the lamps are burning, he's been known to shadow her for six entire blocks. But only down the side streets, where the lighting's not so good.

Her songs are supposed to be tremendously vulgar. Really it's not proper for Grete to go see that sort of thing.

Axel doesn't imagine that I have any intention of resuming our affair. He's wrong about that. Back then it was more or less a—a necessity. I couldn't help it, he was famished and I'm sure I didn't estrange him from Grete. Everyone thinks they have a model marriage. And when I—see them together I believe it myself. But I recall a strange slackening in frenzied moments, a vague fear of his naked lips, an abandon that was nothing but betrayal.

All summer long I was happy to drink tea with Axel.

No, no, no, I'll never go driving with him again. Because that's when I risk falling in love, in lust, losing my head.

There he sits, broad and assured and poised, a pipe in his mouth, ridiculous leather gloves, a sudden lurch, and we drive into a ditch, a pair of horses, a house swarming with kids. But the pipe stays in his mouth, now and then he spits out the window, even that looks good on him.

Meanwhile the days have turned unnaturally warm, scalding October fog torn by the sun, the sudden gleam of a few red leaves, burning roads and bare brown farmland.

I was all aflutter today, went home from the library half an hour early because I was expecting—the fur. Once it had finally, finally come, I turned on all the lamps, a soft enticing light—I'd decided to hurry and have the rooms painted, and there's a new ceiling lamp too.

Oh—Grete wouldn't recognize me. My hair lies so smooth, so matter of fact. I looked at myself in the window pane because the mirror was too small.

Really and truly, I'm tall in this fur, outstretched and haughty, hands sunk in the deep pockets, elbows akimbo.

A pity, though, that I can't look at myself for long. My eyes—aswim in the dark pane—send back a wave of cold and ice.

I'm wearing the fur as I write. I nestle my face in its grey warmth. I appeal to myself, but I don't like me.

It occurs to me that even back in school there was nothing Ulla wanted more than a fur.—Not because it's posh, she used to say, but it's not only the bourgeoisie that doesn't want to freeze!

However tough she may be, Ulla's quick to feel the cold. She has such pale cool skin, she never tans, even in the summer. Maybe because the consulting room with the leather couch never got any sun all year long. That wasn't toughening up, that was murder. And as long as she lives Ulla will never feel warm.

A steam heating pipe passes through her room at the hospital. Naturally, the same heating system passes through the chief physician's room too. In the morning, the same warmth envelops his limbs and hers. But they rarely see each other, sometimes he asks her a question at a patient's bedside, he's very restrained and very polite, especially with the female staff.

Yesterday I saw him in the corridor again. I come to see Ulla quite often these days, and I time my visits to run into him. He has such narrow, colourless lips, but his mouth must have some kind of colour. I'd like to see him smile.

If I were sick—but oh, the patients here have such ghastly diseases, but still, if I were sick, lying in one of those wards, in a white bed with a black chart over it, and he came, then he'd have to come, you see, come to me too, and I'd say something nonsensical, something like Anette did to make Doctor Alexander laugh—

But no, that wouldn't work, I'm sure I couldn't think of anything to say. If I were serious about getting near him, I'd have to become a doctor, go to medical school.

Even as a little girl, Ulla was bent on studying medicine. After all, her bed smelled of iodoform. And yet there was a time when she wanted anything, anything but that—the time that followed the huge disgrace.

I remember it well, it was the talk of the town, the papers ran Ulla's father's picture and even mentioned a young daughter . . . . studying medicine . . . . . may have been present when . . . .

It was the girl G. E., of course. Not the one I'd eavesdropped on from the next room, lying on the mattress, nonsense, we were still in school then and Ulla hid the newspaper in the atlas—

It was a different G. E., a girl who hadn't stayed silent, who'd divulged everything on her deathbed. Ulla's father was thrown in jail. A newspaper spoke of the 'aged doctor's inconceivable moral depravity'.

I didn't go to see Ulla when it happened. I'd just had my appendix out and was in hospital, we were in our third semester—

Yes, right, I was studying history and German, and even then Papa wasn't what he used to be, retired and ill. We moved to a more modest place, Mama said I'd have to think about earning money too, even then she started wearing gloves that weren't chamois and we had just one maid and at dinner one single light bulb shone over the table and I was ill, as I said, purulent appendicitis, I couldn't go see Ulla—

Though I knew she was gritting her teeth and pacing up and down in the room, the operating room, where nothing was left but the leather couch and a certain chair, everything else had been cleared out by the men from the court. There was nothing left in the house, not a piece of paper they hadn't rummaged through, even Hermann's letters from America. They were probably filed away with the rest of the 'evidence', the books and bills that exposed everything, even the long-ago case of the girl G. E.

Ulla paced up and down in the room. She was wearing one of her father's yellow coats, with a few blood spatters, maybe that was 'evidence' too—forty-one cases, they said in court. Forty-one, oh, there must have been many more. If those forty-one had been in the room now, just those forty-one, starved, crippled, with festering holes in their chins and cheeks, with voracious eyes, voracious bony little hands—then her father never would have had to go to jail.

It hadn't been nice, no oh no. And it hadn't been nice when Ulla had to get up one night and crawl under the covers with one of her brothers because a woman, half-dead from loss of blood, was put to bed on her leather couch. That woman stayed for two days and two nights. When she left, weeping and grateful, she pressed a grimy banknote into Ulla's father's hand. It wasn't much. And it wasn't nice that he took it. It wasn't nice at all that he accepted grimy banknotes. None of it was nice. Niceness is a luxury. But goodness, a little goodness, even if you get a bit of grimy money for it, that's something even the poor can manage.

Oh, it was an ugly childhood. Her father, that quiet, kind father with the gentle rabbinical beard, never said an ugly word. But it was ugly all the same—the red plush, the humour magazines, the terrified women. That's why Ulla always had to do callisthenics, had to swim and climb to light-filled heights. That's why she wanted a consulting room in a cheerful, sunny villa one day, a room where nothing illegal would happen. That was cowardly, but it simply couldn't be done any more, you couldn't spend your life terrified to open the newspaper every day—And she didn't want to take any money from her patients, she'd send bills on printed forms, or just wave her hand dismissively—that would be nice, yes, nice, but now that was never to be.

Her father ended up in jail, her oldest brother joined Hermann in America. And Ulla was supposed to come too. No, that wouldn't do. Who was supposed to be there when their father got back? The other two brothers were so unreliable. One was on the road selling stockings, the other fancy-goods. And there was no more money in the house.

No, Axel knows nothing about that whole story, and I'll take good care not even to allude to it. He doesn't like hearing sad things, and he has a confounded respect for anything to do with the law. He's a schoolmaster's son from a German factory town, his mother was supposedly from Denmark, or maybe Norway. That's why he's so thrifty, they're all like that up north. And Axel can't stand it when a woman's life isn't in perfect working order, it's as repugnant to him as a badly set table. He just gets up from the table and leaves.

With Ulla nothing worked, not from the very beginning it didn't. And if he knew about that harrowing winter that followed the huge disgrace, he wouldn't even want to sit next to her.

But my fur's nice. Looks fabulous in his car. I love to smell his leather jacket. It doesn't just smell of leather, it smells of wind, rain and pipe tobacco. Incidentally, he enthused about my fur.

Wait, that's too idiotic. I can't sleep, I've got to get back up, I feel as if I'd forgotten something. What's all this about cars, furs, leather jackets—Damn it, if Grete were to read that, Grete or Anette, they'd probably think I bought the fur for his sake. And that when it's beyond me how to pay the rent this month.

So, just so there's no misunderstanding: I didn't buy the fur for Axel's sake. But for the fur's sake I went driving with Axel today, though I'd made up my mind to cancel. Grete can't go driving at all, she can't take the jolts. I went driving with Axel for the fur's sake, because Axel matches it perfectly, yes indeed, he matches it better than a fragrant bunch of violets.

Who's that laughing? Oh God, don't laugh, anything but that, life's a solemn affair in those white corridors and the chief physician's sleeping. His mouth is frightfully folded up. I know a bit about that mouth. I won't—write—about that.

But the stranger appeared in the library today, lounging in the corner by the window, talking to Herr Zaunegger. She had weary, red-painted lips. Fräulein Marschall stabbed her to death with her googly eyes.

Ulla wouldn't talk to Herr Zaunegger's type.

Today I went to Anette's mother to have my hair washed. I hadn't even realized that she was still in business, she gave up the salon ages ago, but she'd told me her new address when she brought me the ticket.

A sad storefront near the train tracks in an outlying district. Instead of brilliantine, it smells of soot and garlic. No peroxide blondes, no fat gentlemen. The shop is completely deserted. On Saturdays one of the toil-worn neighbours might come and bed her headscarf on the sole, splintered wicker chair.

Nor does Anette's mother have that cinnabar shock of hair any more. Her hair's a play of many colours, brown, green and purple. And the top half of her dentures is missing.

But she still goes on about becoming self-reliant. Anette, now—an utterly unacceptable profession, singing idiotic things and drinking champagne with horrid men, or maybe even plain old red wine. No thank you! But when a woman is self-reliant, like you for instance, enjoying everyone's respect, maybe even esteem, plus room and board at the hospital—

Believe it or not, she's confusing me with Ulla. I could have told her that I work at the library, not the hospital, but then it's not actually that big a difference. Nor is it as far a leap as she thinks, from the library to the cabaret. That chief physician, that Herr Zaunegger and those . . . We all live off men, each in her own way. Only Anette's the least squeamish. She reaches out and grabs. Even as a child. Her fingers were tentacles, red, innocent tentacles.

It's ridiculous that we don't start by learning in school how things stand with women. It ought to be part of the history curriculum. All Doctor Alexander ever talked about was battles and politics and geography, but he never explained how a woman's supposed to lead her life, what she has to do to—well, to drive up her price.

Grete was always the priciest one of us. She does what she's told, nurses the baby and draws up menus with the cook in the blue-and-white striped kitchen. Sometimes she's a bit sad, worried that the price wasn't right after all—

Even as a kid Anette never had a penny in her pocket. She'd buy horrid bonbons and share them straight off with the class, and now she tosses away her caresses, her impudent kisses.

But Ulla—Ulla's shameless. She doesn't want to be bought. She goes around choosing men, handsome, tall, healthy men, idiotically healthy men—she's got no shame at all.

I can't bear having Axel remind me of the past. I don't want to hear any talk of those three months. I don't want to think about that time of regular caresses.

He thinks he can seduce me. Let him go ahead and try!

Ulla has never been seduced. When she went to see Hermann in his student room, she was set on being rid of a torment and an irksome curiosity. When she lived with a young colleague in her first year of medical school, she dictated their Sunday excursions and the colour of his neckties. And then, when she found herself out on the street one night, on a wet and slippery street, famished, embittered, prepared to do anything, cars sliding past her like bloodthirsty monsters, then—

No, Axel mustn't ever get wind of that story. Ulla wouldn't even tell Hermann, if he came back from America, and certainly not the chief physician, if he finally, finally invited her to his room to talk to her in a different way than merely as a member of the female staff.

It's always embarrassing to start a thing and fail to carry it through. Always shameful to realize too late that there's something you can't, you simply can't do. I wouldn't even be writing about it—I'm tired and sleepy anyway. Tomorrow we're supposed to go watch Anette at the cabaret, what a bore, it'll probably go on for half the night, so, well, I wouldn't mention it any more, but Ulla, Ulla's always one for having things out and telling all. She calls it working things off. Maybe it'll even do her good to have it set down here black and white.

So, she was walking down one of those endless uniform Berlin streets where the trees stand like grenadiers and every single sign embodies forbidding slick efficiency. Four weeks after the huge disgrace. So far she'd managed to stint and scrape by, but today the landlady had turned her out of doors—

Ulla's only coat was for summer, dyed dark-brown, and underneath her dress had suddenly gone to pieces, all its folds split like countless fish mouths gaping. The people she asked for work barely bothered to reply, they'd just look at her coat, a brief glance and that was it.

That was how she ended up out on the street one night. Her stomach was a dried-up hole. You're liable to die in a state like that, but Ulla didn't want to die. They'd just locked up her father, cleared out the flat, rifled through every last scrap of paper. And she should do the bastards the favour of croaking on a street corner while their red automobile eyes slid past?

Then someone said:—Hey, doll! A couple of them had said that already. This one had square shoulders and she went along with him. He hooked his arm through hers. A yellow pug nose and inquisitive mouse teeth.—Dinner first, Ulla said.

—You're a right one! He shook his head disapprovingly like a schoolmaster. Scrutinized her under a streetlamp. Then took her to the next beer parlour.

Ulla ate a pair of wieners and another pair of wieners and a bit of salad and a roll and another roll. He went on shaking his head. No manners. The whole time she never even looked at him.

Suddenly he put his hand down on hers. A moist hand, the thumb joint standing out like a hook.—Enough! Let's get going.

Silently they slunk through the rain. He didn't fancy her at all. She'd taken him in. But all those wieners, the salad, the rolls—You don't pay that kind of tab for nothing. She owed him.

Yes, Ulla owed him. She knew that herself. But what exactly, what did she owe him? Her stomach spasmed as if pinched by oily tongs. The salad! What the devil does the fellow want. She's game for anything, but there's something she, she, that clever Ulla's forgotten . . . .

It hit her once she was standing in a room with a grandfather clock, purple flowered wallpaper and separate pot-bellied conjugal beds. Embroidered slippers by the nightstand, a grey cotton nightshirt hanging in the corner.

—My wife's away, he said, already in suspenders.

Ulla thought: Well, I spent two semesters doing dissections. Cadavers aren't very nice either. Nasty to touch. Stinky. And he did pay the tab. Two pairs of wieners, rolls, salad and—

Then he grabbed her, and she lost her mind. The heart-shaped purple glass lamp rained shards over the conjugal beds, chairs smashed, Ulla scratched and bit as though she'd gone berserk, lashed out at a lewd bloated face, felt the hook of the thumb joint, lashed out at the inquisitive mouse teeth, spat and spat—He seized her by the wrists, pug nose snorting.—Lay off, willya! I'll haul you off to the police . . . . . . He trembled, trembled with rage and fear. Voices piped up next door. The wife's nightdress hung in the corner. With one kick, he turned her out of doors. She crouched behind a barrel in the back yard until the front door was unlocked in the morning.

But she didn't head straight out. First she searched the stairwell for the door from last night: Karl Kmunke, Senior Auditor. She noted down the address. She owed him money. Wieners, bread and salad and the broken conjugal lamp. He got it, too.

Ulla's decent, you see, decent to the bone. To this very day she's ashamed about that man, on account of having deceived him. She'd never deceive a man, even if she loves them twenty at a time. But there has to be something for Ulla to love, even if it's just a leather jacket, a whiff of petrol, a cheerful boyish laugh. She won't let herself be bought.

Reading what I wrote today, I feel much better, I can't say how much better I feel. It's not such a shameful story after all. From what I wrote, it's quite clear that Ulla was acting in a kind of hunger-induced psychosis. And men are revolting, so long as they're not the type to fall in love with. You're liable to fall in hate with them when they're standing there in suspenders next to pot-bellied conjugal beds. Fall in hate, that's the way to put it. And the next time Herr Zaunegger puts his hand—he's got long floppy fingers like dead white worms—next time he comes draping those worms over my neck while I'm working at my desk—well, I'm going to clobber him, even if they kick me out of the library. Then I'll just have to do without the health insurance and the pension fund.

Funny, my fur, my beautiful new grey fur smells of leather. Fall in hate or fall in love. I wrote that myself. Of course, who but me? So I'm the one who's in love with Axel, hopelessly in love.

Tonight we're going to go see Anette at the cabaret.

I shouldn't have gone, I had misgivings the moment the hairdresser came with the ticket. But after all, Anette was our classmate. Anette? What's Anette to me?

I was just about to tear up the ticket and toss it in the wastebasket when Axel came to pick me up in his car, his solid healthy car. Grete huddled in one corner, very pale, in a black fur. She has such a wary way of giving me her hand these days. Just as you're about to squeeze it, she's withdrawn it already.

Lord, how that woman bores me! Why is she the one I've been friends with since childhood? There were other girls in the class, Gerda Lange, Liselotte Meller . . . .

We drove down the mild, trickling streets. What kind of a winter is this. Eternally warm and hazy. You get a proper yearning for crystalline snow.

Axel must be insanely bored with Grete. Always sick, always needing rest, exactly as if she were constantly pregnant.

He can go bore himself to death with Grete as far as I'm concerned. I won't interfere. After all, it's his affair. But if Anette, Anette with her bacilli-squirting Chinese eyes, her red tentacle fingers, if she—

What's that to me? When you're in love with a man, with his blond litheness, the automotive way he moves, you've got to—

No, I won't allow it. I won't let him get some disease on me. I won't let his blood be poisoned, his healthy warm blood with the regular pulse.

One day recently when I was lurking in the corridor, waiting for the chief physician, a girl in a hospital pinafore slipped past. She had flaxen hair, a broad face, a blackness about the mouth—She was very young, she smiled like a child. Maybe she was one of Horky's daughters.

When Anette sings, she also has that black tinge. Ulla's a doctor, Ulla could list every single symptom of that type of disease. I can't do that, but I know—

And what's more, three tables behind us sat a girl with colourless hair and a nun's docile smile, the stranger.

How should I bear it, how should I explain? At a table with a yellow balloon, there we sat, me, yes, me, Axel, Grete, me, and Anette was standing onstage in front of us.

All around there were ghastly Cubist daubings on the red walls. Anette's mother sat up in front with a hydrogen peroxide blonde.

Anette's very first hydrogen peroxide torch song made me so nervous that I up and ran away. It was smotheringly hot. Axel isn't quite at ease in a tuxedo.

Then came a lobster-red Negro song with vulgar moves. Axel smirked. The way men do smirk. That made me apoplectic.

But then came the Chinese song. Anette as a Chinese kid, yellow, with slanty eyes, diseased yellow fingers. I looked at Axel. He was leaning forward as if he were moving a 100 km/hour. And Anette yanked her mouth open, there was a blackness around that mouth . . . .

I'll warn Axel. No, that's Ulla's job. Ulla's the doctor. I'll beg Axel, implore him, go down on my knees—I want to kiss his eyes, move down the short straight bridge of his nose on into the corners of his roguish mouth.

Ah yes, it's always the same old story, I know, three whole months, all summer long I was his lover, maybe even his wife, but I'm so impatient I can't hold out, red waves dance before my eyes, I'm dizzy—

I've never once given Axel a real kiss.

Now everything's straightened out, everything's sorted properly and sensibly. I have a bit of a chill. Maybe a sniffle coming on. Maybe— Everything's so right that it gives me the creeps. And I mustn't forget why I'm writing all this down. It's supposed to be, for God's sake, it's supposed to be my life story. What's it turning into?

A well-kept face in the mirror, cream and powder, the lips carefully outlined in red, the room empty and the stranger in the library.

Where . . . . where am I? Where was I this afternoon? What was I doing?

Hush, hush! Reason and logic should suffice to explain it all. Axel picked me up from the library. That wouldn't have been so strange in itself. If only I hadn't had those crazy fears about Anette.

Naturally, he'd been to the barber again because he hadn't shaved that morning. I hate it when men go to barber shops. And he smelled of some nasty soap and shopboy eau de cologne.

That wouldn't normally have caught my attention, but I remembered Anette's mother, her old hair salon, it always smelled like that in there, I saw the rayon curtain, tentacled flowers, and I made up my mind to warn him.

It takes an expert for that. Ulla, in other words. I came up with some foolish alibi, it doesn't matter what, and so we went to see Ulla.

I was going to turn the conversation towards certain diseases, which wasn't hard to do in that hospital, etcetera . . . .

Ulla wasn't in her room. The nurse said she was assisting with an operation, it would be half an hour at most.

Then we were alone. I opened the window. The air hung over the hospital garden like grey dense cotton wool hiding an infinitely distant sleepy evening sun. Soft and filled with secret snow.

Right now, Ulla was assisting the chief physician, obeying his every movement, every blink. Gleaming instruments, ether, chloroform. Ulla was assisting the chief physician. I don't know how it happened, but suddenly I had on the white coat that hung on the door, and I was sitting next to Axel. Suddenly I was kissing him, kissing him with big wild lips, kissing him for the very first time.

And then he leaned forward. 100—120 km/hour in his bright little unerring eyes.

And I loved him, loved him with my teeth and the tips of my fingers, I sucked my way into him, I savoured his powers, his boyish powers—steered them, stroked them.

Somewhere, some time I'd lain on a rumpled bed in a student's dark room, filled with rage and knowledge. Brown olives, salty oily olives.

And then a regatta, a sailing regatta on the open sea, the men slink around the boats like beasts of prey, veering, vaulting—while I dive into the water slim and white like an arrow, spuming seafoam, in the front boat a man wrenches the sail around.

And in the next room a tall blond man clears his throat, the second assistant physician, Doctor N. N., the colleague from next door.

But then suddenly I was standing in the door, while the stranger leaned flushed and abashed against the window, a nun whose veil had been torn off.

I knew everything—oh, how could I not know it?

Ulla served us tea and sandwiches. She didn't touch a thing herself. And I sat there, sat beside Axel and thought of the chief physician limping down the white corridors. I'd like to see him smile just once.

Now I'm Axel's beloved. No, I'm not Axel's beloved. Axel is my boyfriend. That's a big difference.

And I'm not deceiving Grete. I'm deceiving Ulla. That's a difference too.

In fact, I'm stealing from her. I'm stealing her life from her body. Isn't that murder? I'm kissing Axel with her kisses. Isn't that worse than murder?—

I swear, that's not what I wanted. It's not what I want. I'm afraid. It started with Horky. Then there were the others. Grete. Ulla. When will it be Anette's turn? It's getting worse and worse. Someone's looking at me slantwise. Slantwise looks from all the mirrors. I can't see myself from the front any more.

It's winter, crystal-hard, piercing winter. I sleep with the windows open. So what if my temples ache in the morning?

I'm working long hours. At the library they're beginning to take notice of me. Axel tells me about every experiment, every lecture he's going to give. It all sounds quite accomplished, he really knows his stuff. He's no genius, though. He's a wonderful chauffeur. On his own he couldn't invent the least little lever.

I daresay I'm feeling good. We see each other regularly. I don't visit Grete at all any more. It's better that way. My life is tidy. Axel is a prop that I need for that life.

Ulla is hounding me. No, I'm definitely not imagining it. She's always there. Or phoning me. What on earth does she want? She bothers me. There's something questioning in her eyes, it's as though the ice water has melted. Surely I haven't done anything to hurt her? When I mention her to Axel, it's always with the greatest respect. I never allude to the business with her father. Axel's so narrow-minded about such things. He thinks all women lead lives like Grete's, simply sending for the midwife to tend to them at home. Gentle and unattainable, even up to their necks in life's strain and hardship. I'd never tell him about those days in Berlin.

That wretched business with Herr Kmunke and his suspenders wasn't the worst of it, not by a long stretch. Ulla was hungry, that was all. The idea of getting some Kmunke to save your life on some Berlin street hardly seems so unnatural then. You couldn't explain a thing like that to Axel. He's never had to starve.

But maybe the chief physician has. The chief physician has sharp-edged colourless lips, barely parts them when he speaks. But if I should ever see him smile, dear lord, I'll go mad, because—

No, I won't write it, I won't write it. There are things you can't write. I don't want to know about it.

Then I'd better write about something else entirely. Why not about Berlin. That business with the journalist, Herr—no, leave out the name! You needn't bare yourself down to every last detail. Everyone knows his name. Oh, he's a famous writer. You smell greenish slime between the lines of newsprint. He's very shrewd, has lots of money. Extortions.

The worst thing is: Ulla didn't absolutely have to go see him. Hermann had sent her money from America, money to last her for eighteen days. She had no cause to go to Herr—let's say Herr X. Y.

Ulla had a letter from her father to give the man, because they'd gone to school together. Maybe he could give her a job. Stenography and typing at the editorial office. Maybe she could even be his secretary.

Herr X. Y.'s secretary! No, you couldn't even tell the chief physician a thing like that. Much better to be a 'doll' for one night with Senior Auditor Kmunke. After all, what are Herr Kmunke's pot-bellied conjugal beds compared with the poison of a bribed newspaper. To come right out with it: Ulla failed this time too. But this time, too, the disgrace is that she made the attempt.

The chief blame lies with Otto Weber's Mourning Emporium. Practically every day, Ulla would take the train to the employment agency. For forty-five minutes she'd ride through the hellscape of sooty back-buildings with tiny little balconies and curtains, yes indeed, curtains in the windows. These buildings are jumbled together as though spewed aside from some evil cavalcade. Sometimes a homely lamp's still shining down on a senile spectre in an armchair, women in night-jackets stand at the window, but no, they're not about to hurl themselves onto the train tracks, they're fixing their hair in the murky panes, baby things to wash—

Oh, it's unbearable! But all you need to do is look away, and you see the gigantic black posters for Otto Weber's Mourning Emporium, mourning manufactured cheaply, oh so cheaply, by the dozens, by the hundreds. All you need to do is switch off the homely lamp, yank back the curtains, avert your gaze from the murky panes and—

Those you leave behind can get what they need at Otto Weber's Mourning Emporium.

After one of those rides, after carrying her father's letter in her purse for weeks, Ulla, suddenly and without thinking, went to see editor-in-chief X. Y. She had her old dyed summer coat on. What harm could it do? After all, he and father had gone to school together. Two poor Jewish boys in a small Polish town.

'This is the entrance for ladies and gentleman.' The concierge eyed her suspiciously. Well, 'lady' certainly didn't apply to Ulla.

Besides, she was menstruating. That always gives her porcelain skin a slightly parched tinge. It was cold. She was having cramps.

The chambermaid's suspicion. Warm carpets. The letter is being delivered. Waiting in a smotheringly soft, smotheringly luxurious room, silken cushions. Walls of books.

Then Ulla was sitting across from a man—I can't recall if his eyes were grey or blue, if he had a long or short nose, if he was big or small, maybe he was wearing a velvet smoking jacket. But his lips were reptiles, naked, slick, wriggling reptiles.

Ulla couldn't speak. Again she smelled the green slime between the lines of newsprint. She felt sick.

And Herr X. Y. scrutinized her. No, not with his eyes, with his lips. And the reptiles said: Why do you look so bad? A woman mustn't look bad, ever.

And the reptiles wriggled over the dyed summer coat, crawled through the tattered frock's gaping fish mouths. The slip, the slip, she'd gone five days without changing her slip, Ulla, the best gymnast, the best swimmer in the whole class.

Oh, Senior Auditor Kmunke had at least valued her at a couple of wieners, rolls and salad, but this one, this Herr X. Y. instantly reckoned her value as virtually nil. She'd come looking for work. A woman mustn't ever look bad.

I don't know what words were exchanged. She sat very still in front of him, barely replying. She yearned for a long, infinitely long hypodermic needle. You don't battle with reptiles. You exterminate them.

But it's better, a thousand times better to leap from a curtained window in front of a train, a locomotive, straight into the maw of Otto Weber's Mourning Emporium, than to seek help from a—well, from a Herr X. Y.

Soon after that Ulla wrote me a despairing letter. And what did I do—I simply went to *Herr von* . . . and touched him for money. He was astonished enough to give me a respectable sum. Oh, fiddlesticks, if you can go to editor-in-chief X. Y. to ask for a job, you can go to some *Herr von* . . . and ask him for money. I was his sister-in-law, after all. We were sitting across from each other at the card table and I told him something about gambling debts. I almost think that impressed him.

Back then Bea played insane amounts of bridge and poker. Why shouldn't I lose money once in a while too?

Incidentally, we were having a miserable time of it then. Papa had just died, and Mama moved in with Bea. The only way I could continue my studies was to give lots of lessons, and I found myself the fifth-floor room where I still live today, only instead of the wallpaper with alpine woods and bridges crossing mountain torrents there's now a smooth sand-yellow wall. It was a grey time. When I went to visit Mama one Sunday, she had a letter from Uncle Max. From Liverpool. Undated.

It was just a few words. Oh Papa! Papa had the same shoulders as Uncle Max, the same cautious, angular movements of the elbows. Papa! They'd buried him in the ground. And Bea had children with that *Herr von* . . . . The oldest one wasn't quite right in the head. Papa had had so many worries in his last years. And Mama had grown old, white hair—

I flung my arms around her neck and wept. I wept for her and Papa, for Bea and her children, for the salty shining North Sea afternoon when Uncle Max vanished on a ship. And maybe I was crying for myself.

Since then I hadn't cried once.

But today tears shot into my eyes, hot and despairing. I couldn't see, I steadied myself on the white radiator in the white corridor.—Meanwhile I'm sure the white-dressed girl with the pail of disinfectant has come to wipe away my tears.

In a hospital everything's so uncaring. But Axel mustn't come to me today, not today, just this once, I can't stand it when he laughs with his solid smoke-stained teeth.

Just not today!

Well then, he's not coming. He was a bit surprised when I cancelled. But what's this? My tears are flowing again. There's nothing to be done, it can't be kept secret any longer: I saw him smile.

I was coming down the corridor, murky snow-light behind murky windows, and there he stood, talking to a patient. Such a young thing, maybe fourteen years old, dark in her striped hospital pinafore, slit eyes. Anette? No, not Anette. Perhaps her sister? Anette doesn't have a sister.

And he was smiling! Lively wrinkles across his cheeks, his eyes filled with sweet kind light, his colourless lips drawn apart in animation, but in between—dead teeth, big, dank, dead. A set of false teeth.

I hated his mother. It was her fault he'd fallen off a table as a child. She sent him off to school without enough sandwiches. He went hungry. No one looked after him. At the age of ten he was already wrecked.

Oh, I want to steal my way in to him, to his room, where his bed is, where his socks are kept. I want to cuddle him.

I want to be tender with him, infinitely tender. I've never been tender with anyone before.

But I can't go in to him. I belong to the female staff.

The female staff—what's that supposed to mean! Yes, Herr Zaunegger's female staff. He's starting to get angry at me, by the way. While Fräulein Marschall is turning quite friendly. Today she offered me some of her thermos tea. Just the sight of the thermos made me queasy.

Altogether I've been feeling sick quite often. And Axel is constantly coming to see me. Today he smelled of a certain shopboy eau de cologne again. The chief physician doesn't use eau de cologne at all. Only pale unscented soap.

—What's the matter with you? he asked. I wasn't nice to him at all. To Axel, that is. He doesn't need me, really. Grete makes sure his socks are darned. Buys him new ones.

His car is at the shop. Recently when I was lying next to him, he was breathing so beautifully, so deep, so sated, and I was stretched out full length, almost tall on my back—I longed to crawl inside him, in under his arm. Dwindling into a little girl. It's so hard to be a woman. And a clever woman, at that.

Oh, I'm not so clever at all, I'm a silly goose. And at this rate, by summer Herr Zaunegger will scheme to get me kicked out of the library. I wouldn't put it past him.

Besides, I feel wretched. As though I'd been nailed shut. Constant bouts of nausea. Just yesterday I had to leave work early again. I'd rather be at home, alone. If only it weren't for Ulla! Showing up at my doorstep this evening to bring me tangerines. How did she know about my craving for tangerines?

And I know one day she'll look at me with her ice-water eyes and say—

No, no, no, I don't want to hear it! I am, after all, I am, Herr Zaunegger notwithstanding, I am still the librarian with the pension fund. I'm self-reliant, I know what I want, what I'm going to do. I'm certainly not that girl G. E.

Ulla, now she'd know what to do. You could say she's been learning since childhood. Faugh, it's mean to write that. But Ulla was always mean to herself. When she took her first dive, she felt sick as a dog, but then she dove right back into the pool. The others clapped, yelled bravo, no one noticed a thing. And it was no small feat to come back from Berlin as a penniless failure and then go on to study medicine despite the disgrace. Ulla went through with it. She never did go easy on herself.

She wouldn't go easy on herself at a time like this either. Wouldn't miss a day on the job. No one would guess how wretched she feels. Not even the chief physician.

Good heavens, why does everything have to turn out the way you always knew it would! On the day when the article about the girl G. E. was tucked away in the atlas, in the middle of the map of England or Brazil or Scandinavia, that day I knew it was bound to turn out as it did. Why did it have to be the girl G. E.? I laid my head on my arms on the polished school desk. Inside me's all the terror, all the dread of the stranger who'd bled to death, yes inside me. My poor dried-up breasts, where will my baby drink?—and I smelled meat broth.

That meat broth! That was how I knew right away. The whole city's cooking meat broth now. It's unbearable. Axel—

No, I mustn't think about Axel. Mustn't see him and above all, mustn't smell him. Yesterday I looked into the mirror after—but why write down such nasty things?—Well, I looked into the mirror and I saw his impudent little boyish eyes all foolishly and inquisitively startled, a blond face.

I'll take the mirror down. There's no need for mirrors on the walls. Mirrors are pictures. Constantly changing, unbearably new pictures.

The strange girl is gone. Doesn't even come to the library any more. I don't like the stranger, I fear her. But I yearn for her.

Ulla's to blame, Ulla alone is to blame for it all. If I'm ever hauled off to court, it wasn't me, that's all, I decline all responsibility, I don't know a thing.

Well, Ulla looked at me with her pitiless ice-water eyes and said:—This time it's really true. What are you going to do?

I felt like slapping her in the face, we were sitting in the streetcar across from each other, but you can't do that, not in front of everyone. Besides, I don't know if I could even make myself slap Ulla in the face.

I didn't reply. But when she said:—Let's go see Axel, I went along. In fact, I'm always 'going along'. That's the tragedy.

Ulla was very pale. Despite all the cream and powder. I sensed it, and trembled.

What does Ulla have to do with it. Ulla, Ulla! It's not like I'd taken something she'd want to have back.

Axel wasn't home, but Grete was. Ulla knew that ahead of time, Ulla wanted it that way, she was counting on it. Ulla's so clever. Too clever.

The day after tomorrow I'll be lying in hospital.

Axel wasn't home. But that was no reason for it to be so empty, even on the stairs. Practically dead. The whole house smelled of rotting flowers. The clock in the living room had stopped. A forgotten book lay open on the mantlepiece. And it was cold.

The housemaid told us that Grete was in bed. She wasn't feeling well, but we should wait, she'd come soon.

Waiting for Grete. With Axel away. Grete—what kind of a name is that, anyway? Grete? Faded days of childhood. One time Uncle Max led Grete with his hairy hand to a circle of playing children. And then we were all standing in a cemetery, drunken March sun, jaunty tulips, hyacinths—And Grete lay in bed in this cold, dead house, lay cold and dead amid luxurious lace pillows, the windows curtained, without even tulips or hyacinths, just a remote withered water-lily scent.

Grete! Ulla leafed in the book in front of the fireplace. Grete—what is that? For weeks, for months I'd forgotten Grete utterly. And now she was lying dead on her bed. For God's sake—

No, she wasn't dead. She walked into the room, gentle and pale. She was wearing a quiet lavender-coloured frock and she smiled with broad white teeth and she turned on the lamp over the little tea table and she had the maid make a fire in the fireplace.

—It's awfully cold, she said. She shivered. She wasn't dead. The lamp burned under its silk shade. The flames flickered in the fireplace. But it didn't get any warmer.

Then came the tea and then—the Devil only knows what that was about. Ulla's so confoundedly clever and Ulla took me with her to Grete. But she can't be so cunning, so sneaky that she knew it all ahead of time.

And yet, when the maid brought the tea (by the way, that maid bore an odd resemblance to the stranger), when the maid brought the tea, Ulla smiled. Just for a moment, perhaps a tenth of a second. I saw it in the mirror over the fireplace, I saw her white rapacious teeth—

No, nothing happened, nothing at all. Grete and I didn't pounce on each other, we didn't yell, we didn't even cry. Ulla didn't need to soothe us, she just smoked countless cigarettes as we had tea.

The tea was light green. Grete said it was Chinese, a friend of Axel's had sent it from Shanghai. A green tea, imagine, a light green tea, redolent of flower petals, slightly rotten, sweet, corpse-pale petals.

I set the cup back down, covered my eyes with my hands. Oh God, oh God, anything not to vomit here, not here in Grete's well-kept salon.

When I looked up, Grete was sitting tall and straight before me. She looked at me with a gaze—No, no, those weren't Grete's eyes, so gentle so understanding, they were Ulla's ice-water eyes. She looked at me, and her gaze was filled with hatred.

What more is there to say? In Grete's presence no talking takes place. We drank the green tea in silence. Once Ulla mentioned Anette. Then the conversation turned to Axel. And Grete told us she was expecting her second child.

I can't murder Grete. I love Axel far too little for that. She'd die without saying a single reproachful word to him. She'd die on the choked-back reproach. But she couldn't bear it if at the same time—she couldn't bear it, even knowing everything. And that's what's so awful.

But Axel doesn't know a thing. And he mustn't know. Of course I could lie, say the baby's from Herr Zaunegger or something horrid like that. But how am I supposed to support it? You can't acquire a baby on the instalment plan like a fur. And I'd be kicked out of the library then and there. Not even the kind chief physician would want to, no, would be allowed to keep me on as a member of the female staff. Women's so-called emancipation, a downright swindle, said Ulla, accompanying me on certain unpleasant errands. Two days from now I'll be in hospital.

Ulla looks terrible. Her eyes are a burning blue. All this is more than she can take. She'd never, ever confess to her chief physician that she was the one who found me the doctor. When she talked to him, she felt sick to her stomach. I wish I'd die when they do it. It's all so ugly. But no, that mustn't happen. Then Ulla might be hauled into court. Who knows if I'd manage to keep mum the way the girl G. E. did.

Two days from now—holy Mary, Mother of God!

Right, Horky always said that prayer with me at bedtime. Hail Mary—she sat on the edge of my bed—Full of grace—her face gleamed as though she'd rubbed it with liquid candlewax—The Lord is with thee—she was wearing a blue apron—Blessed art thou among women—Blessed is the fruit of thy womb—

I always felt afraid of these words. I didn't understand what they meant. They're heavy and pregnant, filled with anxiety and fate. I didn't know what that fruit could be. I always pictured a big yellow pear. But that's the way Horky prayed with me, evening after evening. Her straw-like hair was pulled back taut. That's the way she sat on my bed. Square and solid as a crate.

As the tok-tok of the ether constricted my brain, a spectre rose out of me, slender, cool and porcelain-white. But I faded out on the operating chair, my legs meanly, nastily suspended in the air.

When I opened my eyes, a gentle nurse was bending over me. She adjusted my blanket. Her hands were veined blue, they were light, weightless as air.

Then I took another look at her face. Oh, yes, of course, familiar features. The stranger was bending over my bed. The unreachable girl was very near and filled with terrible pity.

For three days the gentle nurse took care of me. We never spoke. On her lips, like pain, played a smile of consolation. It wasn't meant for me. Who was it meant for? Maybe the unborn child who'd left life unlived.

Oh, this life of ours!

There I lay on a strange bed like an empty sack.

One time a strange lady came through the door. She was holding a bouquet of mimosas. That had to be a mistake. You give flowers to new mothers, but not to—

She came towards me, talking too loudly and wearing too much perfume, and I saw that it was Ulla.

She talked too much. Wondered if she should inform Axel about everything after all? Oh, nonsense, why bother! What business is it of his? And he's got such a childish fear of anything against the law. Besides, it's all over now.

Over—yes over. Ulla went on about all sorts of things. Her eyes roamed the walls, expressionless, God knows what she was thinking. The gentle nurse smiled at her consolingly. I think I fell asleep even before she left.

I shouldn't have written all that down. The whole week that I've been back home, I've felt a strangely tormenting disquiet. I keep losing gloves, books, pencils, everything. And when I look, I never find the right things.

But now that I'm writing again, I know what I'm looking for. The stranger, the stranger, the gentle nurse. That's only natural. I've asked Axel not to see me for a while. Twice, when Ulla came I pretended not to be home. You can't possibly be so alone. You can't possibly be so utterly alone. I can't possibly be. I'm at the point of going on a Sunday jaunt with Herr Zaunegger. Or asking Fräulein Marschall to the movies with me some evening. I can't take it any more.

The room is so empty that I feel the urge to ask for those idiotic Alpine landscapes and mountain torrents that used to adorn the walls. And I need the mirror back. Let the gentle nurse gaze at me. I don't want to live without the stranger. Let her gaze at me with her consoling smile. At me. Because I've left a life unlived as well. A life, just one? A hundred lives, a hundred thousand.

Off to bed, off to bed! If only the blanket didn't stay so cold, as cold as though it covered a corpse. And then there's the soap. The business with the soap is too much to bear. I can wash myself as much as I like. The soap never gets any smaller.

If I'm able to write, to write even today, at this desk, as always, then it can't be a delusion that I, I, the librarian with—

It's impossible that it's not me who wrote all these things, all these scribbled pages, that it's someone else instead, many others, many others or no one at all. I've got a passport, after all, a legally valid signature. I—

But damn it all, who can prove to me that it's I? I? Who's I? If I can't even prove it to myself, then why—

My Lord, who can help me if I can't. Who can explain to me that—it's too awful to put into words—

That the mirror was empty.

This morning I asked the charwoman to hang it back where it was. The light spot on the sand-coloured wall looked just awful, anyway.

And when I came home this afternoon—I went and stood and stared into that spot. The stranger, for heaven's sake, where is the stranger? Not a person, not a face, not a soul crying out. Is Grete dead, has Ulla vanished? Where are Anette, Bea, Horky, and, for that matter, where's Fräulein Marschall?

Surely you can't be all alone in the world, can you? You can't see no one when you look into a mirror.

I threw the mirror down the light shaft. The spot on the wall looks like an empty buttonhole, an eye that's leaked away.

It's unnaturally warm, someone remarked in the library. Fräulein Marschall's wearing a summery white blouse. Axel sent a postcard from Paris. So he's in Paris. I immediately mislaid the postcard. Whatever it said is already forgotten. I'm forgetting everything now. My heart and my blood, strange that I'm still able to wait. What am I waiting for?

7.30 this morning. I was still in bed, an untouched cup of tea beside me. It's so awfully hard to drag myself to the library. And anyway, so what if I don't, then someday someone else will take my place. Fräulein Marschall inspecting her sidelong, all aflutter, Herr Zaunegger running his tongue over his lips—

So, this morning there was a sudden, fierce, impatient knocking at my door and in came a poor girl in worn-out shoes, a matted grey coat, a new salmon-pink straw hat—Yes, a straw hat. So spring is here.

That poor girl was Anette. You see, Anette is poor. In the morning. In the evenings she wears her washable silk stockings and little dance dresses turned inside-out. The blackness around her mouth is—I don't know how else to put it, there's even more of it. In the morning she has rings under her eyes and skin as dull as leather. The rest of the time she probably wears cheap, toxic makeup.

Anette sat on the edge of my bed. She drank my tea and chattered in her slightly tinny voice. All she wanted was a little favour, nothing much at all, a minor matter of the bailiff and pawn tickets at the hair salon, a male friend in a momentary quandary, she'd need just eight days or ten at the most. She'd never have come up with the idea on her own, it was Ulla who sent her.—Ulla. I flinched. I never hear from Ulla any more. But Ulla's thinking of me, Ulla knows everything, knows how everything hangs together, knows it better than I do, anyway. Ulla is clever, too clever, and if Ulla sends Anette to me, she's sure to have her reasons. The money problem is just an alibi, of course. Ulla doesn't seriously think I can help. After all, I'm still deep in debt from the fur.

Oh, that fur! There it is, hanging from the window latch in the shimmering sunlight, grey and downy. I hate it, the whole room smells of leather and petrol, inquisitive grey animals.

—I don't have any money, I told Anette. But you know how to pawn things. If you take that fur to the pawnshop, I'll lend you all the money you want.

Anette let out a peep like a startled bird. A moment later she'd torn open the window, snatched the fur to her body and smoothed it against her with trembling fingers. Her black hair took on a completely new red sheen, like crimson-dyed wool. When she tossed it, the dust motes danced in the sunlight. Anette shimmered all over.

—Hey, she said, that's absolutely grand. She wiped a wet kiss across my cheek and off she went. Her matted coat lay on my table.

At noon she rang me up in the library. She'd just used the fur to make a huge impression on a theatre agent, things were looking up— Gazing into Fräulein Marschall's inquisitive goggle eyes, I asked Anette if she'd go to the movies with me that evening.

I'd absolutely love to. But better make it tomorrow.

It was a strange movie night. Nonsensical and childish. The first childish thing was that I put on Anette's coat. But it looked so warm with its thick fabric—a fabric that seemed puffed up with air, maybe even cigar smoke—and outside it had suddenly turned cold, a caustic storm was sweeping down the street, flinging hard, broad flakes in my face.

But when I saw Anette sitting under shrieking lightbulbs and the poster of an angel-faced woman, I suddenly perked up. She was wearing my fur, which looked bizarrely shaggy on her, the salmon-pink straw hat bobbed away on top, and she was sucking at a chocolate bar that probably had pink cream inside.

Air freshener, bad teeth, poking feet and lily-of-the-valley perfume. That was at first. But then came the adagio from the Ninth

Symphony, breaking waves and Anette closed her big mouth. She took her hat off, bowed her head. What a small head she has, narrow and oval, and when she lets it droop, it resembles a sad grape.

It was an awfully sad movie. The lovers were separated. She was a poor girl, with a mop of crimped curls and a white shirt blouse. But he was a highbred young man, a lord, with nobly chiselled features, marvellous long legs, and a castle on the auction block. Of course, he had to fall into the hands of the elegant black widow, it being imperative to hold on to his ageing mother's familiar home.

Anette blew her nose. Maybe she was crying. The end of the chocolate bar fell to the floor. The beaded purse clinked as it followed. A minor commotion in the audience. That's always happening to Anette. Even in school her pencil sharpener kept rolling practically up to the blackboard, all the girls would turn around, Doctor Alexander would say:—Oh, leave it be, and Anette would giggle.

Anette giggled this time too:—Look at that silly goose, thinking HE's in love with her.

She pronounced that HE with capital letters, and as the lord bowed with perfect form over the demonic widow's hand, palms, Persian carpets, silky pinschers and 'I Lost My Heart in Heidelberg', Anette whispered in my ear, her voice hoarse and redolent of chocolate:—Do you know where HE is now?

—Ssh, went a fat man in front of us.

And I don't know anything about him. Not even if he's alive. He always spent so much time in the mountains, maybe he had a fall.

Anette and I held hands, since we weren't allowed to talk. We trembled as the web of destiny closed in upon the lovers, we started up when He plunged from his horse the day before the wedding, we wiped away our tears when the blonde hastened to his bedside. We wished we could leap into the picture to scratch out her rival's eyes.

Everything turned out all right in the end. Sunshine in the village church, myrtle and lips melding together on an Italian balcony.

Anette smiled blissfully amid the throng of moviegoers tromping to the exit. We walked home, still holding hands. It was cold still, but the storm was over. Anette talked about Doctor Alexander.—For his sake even I could have gone to university.—We kept walking on past my front door, like old times, when Mama scolded me every day because I came home from school so late.

I tossed away the grey cigar-smoke coat. I fell in bed, drugged with sleep. I dreamt about Doctor Alexander. He was standing amid palms and Persian carpets and I was all in a flutter, trying to explain something terribly important. He regarded me with a noble gaze, but a moment later he had to bite back his laughter.

•

Thank goodness Anette drops by so often these days. She's fallen out with her boyfriend, Willy. She usually calls him Herr Willy, he's the son of a mid-sized delicatessen. Sometimes he helps out at the shop, but he doesn't have to, and he's got another girl now for sure.

For sure! Anette kicked her feet when she told me about that. Of course she doesn't care 'that much', and she bit at her cigarette, with her they always have gnawed yellow butts. Usually we go to the movies or a little cafe in the outskirts where Anette has credit. She'd rather not come to my place. She doesn't like it there.—Your flat's so bare, she says. And a couple of days ago she brought me a pair of yellow muslin curtains with maybug-sized polka dots. From her mother's shop, which shut down for good. Now her mother goes around dressing people's hair 'at home'.

I shouldn't have put up the curtains. Ulla would find them utterly unacceptable. They're stifling, that's it, stifling. Now my room doesn't get any nice clear light. But Anette would be mortally offended if I took them down again.

Herr Zaunegger likes Anette's shabby coat, though goodness knows my fur was much nicer for the winter. He runs his hand down my back. Today there were a couple of damp bedraggled snowdrops in a water glass on my desk and Fräulein Marschall told me I'd catalogued a book wrong. She really is a nasty thing!

In my room one of the Alpine torrents with the buxom girl on the swaying footbridge is back up on my wall. But where the mirror used to hang, there's still a gaping hollow pale spot.

It's been two whole days since Anette came to see me. But she lent me a novel she's especially fond of: *The Destiny of Brigitte Helmer*. One of those stories about feminine pride and womanly dignity. Really not very proper for a librarian of practically many years' standing—

Oh, to hell with all that harping on education and intelligence. When I was reading Chapter 15, where the beautiful, gentle Brigitte Helmer, who'd gone to work as a typist for the prominent lawyer Doctor Johannes Rüdiger, was just tidying up her boss's papers and he, the man who's so kind to criminals and the poor, strode past her out of the room without a word because—well, straight away I had to think of Ulla and the chief physician. Ulla isn't quite beautiful and definitely not gentle and Ulla and the chief physician won't get married at the end of the book or rather at the end of their lives, quite apart from the fact that Doctor Johannes Rüdiger doesn't have false teeth and can't possibly limp—

But doesn't it all come down to the same thing? Lying in bed with the novel, a shiver passed through me every time Doctor Rüdiger entered the building. And when Brigitte Helmer went out in the dead of night, hands trembling as she bought a ticket for the next express train, regardless of its destination, anywhere to get away from him—I cried. Big, warm, living tears. Oh, it's grand to cry like that. I lay in bed delicate and untouchable like a marble statue in a lace negligee. Doctor Johannes Rüdiger sat with elbows propped on his ebony desk thinking of Brigitte Helmer, half crazed with yearning and despair.

A good thing no one but me will read these pages in the end. It's disgraceful, all this stuff I'm scribbling. Laughable, almost. But at least it shows me that I'm still capable of crying, that I'm far from not caring, that I, I, yes I am lying in my bed—while Anette's sitting in a bar filled with cold smoke. It's not worth the owner's while to heat any more, the ancient lightbulbs give off a dripping reddish light, couples sit at the little marble tables, sallow youths or elderly gentlemen, the waiters wear stained white jackets, one of them has a blackness about his mouth too.

Anette shivers in my fur. The new straw hat's lying on a pile of fashion magazines and dog-eared humour rags. She's alone with her watery coffee, alone. There's nothing sadder for a woman than being alone.

Sometimes a Herr Director comes, or a shop boy. Then she laughs with her huge mouth, smokes and drinks eggnog. That's business. With Herr Willy, she was even a little bit in love. But this way's fine too.

Love—that has nothing to do with anything. Real love—that's something you'll get from Doctor Johannes Rüdiger, at best. You'd have to be a little baby girl to think love finds you just like that. In school. In school we thought those sorts of things about Doctor Alexander. Every single one of us believed: Today, tomorrow, the day after he'll find some excuse to call me into the staff room, by Christmas at the latest, or the Easter break, and he'll light a cigarette, take my hands in his big mountain-climbing paws and say:—You're the only one I've ever loved.

But Doctor Alexander never took us seriously. He couldn't even be bothered to make a fuss when we cheated on a certain history exam, our honesty and our accomplishments meant as little to him as our childish nightgowns. Only when Grete wasn't there, he'd gaze at her empty seat.

Nor did Axel ever really love Grete. He sees her every day, but he ogles the others. When Anette sang her yellow Chinese song, he'd have let Grete bleed to death beside him just to go and—dear God, certainly not to love that wretched depraved child. It occurs to me that whenever Anette said silly things, Doctor Alexander smirked the way men do, and Herr Zaunegger too, once when it came out that Fräulein Marschall actually had caught me cataloguing a book wrong, he didn't scold, he just—well, he just smirked too.

Ever since I let him kiss me again by the washbasin outside the toilet, my life at the library has been a lot easier. My God, he's not exactly good-looking, and his moustache is ridiculously scraggly. But in the end he smells of shaving soap and cigar smoke like any other man. And he's so stupid! I could turn the library upside-down, stop working entirely or catalogue everything wrong, if I only do the few little things he asks of me.

Oh, that's impossible, I can't believe it,! In the windowpane—there wasn't any knock at the window, was there—I spin around—in the windowpane I see slit eyes and a gleefully grinning mouth, aren't my fingers red?

My God, my God, I'm no longer alone, I'm framed by yellow muslin curtains with pink maybug polka dots.

What luck. What a tiny, modest, filthy-pink bit of luck! Grete, Ulla, the strange girl have abandoned me. But Anette's there, Anette's breathing beside me. What does it matter that her stockings are just washable silk, bottom of the barrel, that she has that ghastly scar on her stomach and darkness about the mouth. She's wearing my fur.

Once she wore genuine, substantial silk underthings with lace and ajour stitching. The rest of us were still in school, and she was working at the lingerie salon, where she had a frightful habit of pilfering. Of course all she could get her hands on was a couple of chemises and a slip that the ironing lady had singed. There was a warm, veiled light in the ladies' changing room, but back where the girls worked, it smelled of refuse from the light shaft and coarse cotton underwear. Why shouldn't little Anette have her fun, when she'd just been kicked out of school? The light green silk combos she'd bought with her first clandestine earnings seemed like tissue paper now. She threw them away. She stuck her nose into the little fitting rooms, devoured the opulent smell of well-kept hips. The ladies were fond of her. One of them gave her an old pair of silk panties once with a spot that wouldn't come out, but those panties had a funny smell, of Quelques Fleurs and something else.

Anette really enjoyed working at the lingerie salon. If she hadn't loved the fragrant stuff enough to pilfer, she could have stayed on with pleasure. What came next was harder.

Does Axel have the least inkling about things like that? I'm sure he thinks a girl takes to the streets for the fun of it. Yes, the fun! And he thinks that if Grete doesn't, it's because Papa and Mama forbade it. When Grete couldn't do it even if she wanted to. Because none of it gives her any pleasure. What a jackass! To think he's never noticed that! And Ulla couldn't, because she gets too much pleasure out of it. Axel hasn't got the slightest notion.

But I gritted my teeth this afternoon with Herr Zaunegger when—Why should I grit my teeth again just to describe it? Incidentally, he's engaged to Fräulein Marschall. Secretly. They're planning to get married when he gets a promotion.

What's that to me! Next Friday I get two sick days off, making it three days including Sunday, and Anette and I are going to go on a trip somewhere. It's so gorgeous out now, meadows full of primroses, hillsides full of spring heather, the midday sun rips the skin from your body. Anette's going to take along a spirit stove. She has the most divine travel slippers, orange with high yellow heels.

Oh, those three days were intoxicatingly bright. Anette wore a pea-green summer dress. She's a completely different person when you see her out in the woods. And those woods! The little firs were sprouting long, green, voracious tips, tips that were sometimes longer than the branches. They looked funny, so hobbledehoy.

And Anette was capable of flopping down in the grass and kicking her feet for sheer pleasure. She found the loveliest sprigs of daphne and her sallow skin turned rust-brown, as if smoked.

The coarse linen of the beds in the inn, white and nubby, held the spring sun. Anette lay in the linen, brown and bare and wanton, as matter-of-factly as she'd lie on a meadow. She pulled me towards her, smelling of hidden daphne. The candles burned uncertainly in a soap dish on the washstand. Anette kissed me. Because, thank God, there was no man who could use her that night. She has such impudent inquisitive fingers.

Outside the window a blooming chestnut beamed.

How does she know these things? She takes each strange body in her hands as if she'd slept beside it night after night in her stained old childhood bed.

The sculptress must have taught her. The sculptress had greenish teeth and the corners of her mouth sagged. She was in the habit of trying on flowing chemises in the muted warm light of the lingerie salon. And sometimes she'd stroke Anette's legs that poke like inquisitive sticks from the threadbare wool skirt. After Anette was caught stealing, she went to the hairdresser and asked for permission to use her daughter as a model.

But she didn't model anything on Anette. Her greedy hands plunged into the clay and shaped animals, always animals. Long, pointed, snarling muzzles, predatory fangs between narrow lips, and antlers, wild, heavenward-straining, nonsensical, cruel antlers. The white studio with the white glass globe lamps was already filled with these animals. Anette felt afraid of them when she stretched out on the tiger skin, smoking opium cigarettes, only now and then stretching a leg in the air, lazy, languid and lustful herself.

It was a terrible time. The sculptress drank frightful quantities of whisky. Sometimes she'd hit Anette and right after that she'd cry and French kiss her. She brought her gifts of Turkish sweets, but I'd still rather go with Herr Zaunegger, even if all he gives me is hazelnut chocolates.

At the library they say he and Fräulein Marschall are going to get married soon. At any rate, Marschall's got her hair cut and bought a new spring coat. Pale grey, porridgey.

Anette's still running around in my fur. Isn't it getting too hot? It's all the same to me. But yesterday—

Now wait a minute, that's exactly what I didn't want to write. I didn't want to write about Axel at all any more. I'd promised myself. But suddenly, right in the middle of things, he slips in on me, standing there in my room, giving me Grete's regards.

Grete—oh, that's another name I never meant to write again.

I can't, I won't think about Axel any more. All at once it hurts terribly.

But it's impossible not to write about him. Today, just today, one last time I have to—

I? In the mirror's stead a hollow hole in the wall. Is it even still me who's writing?

Piles of scribbled pages. Whose—doing—is—all—this?

So there Anette stood, leaning on the opened window's sill, between the polka-dotted muslin curtains, behind her nothing but black summer air and of course she was wearing the fur, but for myself I was ironing an airy frock. We were about to go to the movies or a coffeehouse, maybe a garden concert, when Axel came in and, I'm sure I wasn't imagining things, walked up to her, to Anette, that is, she was wearing my fur—

He was nonplussed. And so was I. So was she, probably.

It was one of those occasional visits he makes to show he's a, how do you put it, a 'decent' person. And those visits were becoming a bit of a bore, only yesterday there was all that excitement.

Of course, the only one to blame is Anette with her childish errand-girl imagination.

Because with Axel sitting on my bed (the only two chairs were holding the ironing board) and Anette furtively gnawing at a cigarette, as I could hear while ironing, I looking down at the dress, it had so overly many tiny pleats, well—No, I can't even write properly any more, Doctor Alexander always used to say: don't get muddled, take your time, and take it easy . . . .

I think I'll start from the beginning. No beating about the bush, the truth will out: That night, for just a few minutes, it was Doctor Alexander sitting on my bed. Our Doctor Alexander. To conceal his indifference he smiled with smoke-stained teeth, almost sheepish, he was naked and red beneath his mountain tan and talked about a climbing tour and his paws groped along my blanket.

Ulla would say:—Why shouldn't Axel talk about a climbing tour too? But Ulla doesn't understand a thing. However clever she may be. Anette, though—Anette looked at him, sitting there in front of her like that. The whole room turned gold like the last act of a revue. He made a sarcastic remark about the muslin curtains. I couldn't go on ironing. It was like being stabbed.

And then came the wicked thing: He invited me over for Tuesday evening, an intimate gathering, Ulla will be there too, a couple of friends, and he kissed my hand and took his leave and didn't see Anette leaning against the window sill, he'd simply forgotten her. He walked out the door, suddenly very tall and filled with terrible power.

Doctor Alexander never took us seriously either. He smirked when Anette said silly things. But as for kindness, now—no one was ever kind to Anette.

Actually, there once was someone, but it was a long time ago and doesn't really count. It was in Anette's circus days, when she bit iron bars in two and held up a bridge and four strong men tromped over it. Anette was all dressed in purple velvet, she wore a curly golden wig and had to paint her brown skin white—that's how the director wanted it. In the glum November fog, they travelled from town to town with three elephants as part of the troupe, and horse manure wherever you stepped.

Anette brought down the house. She would bow with page-like elegance. She'd have made the big time for sure if it hadn't been for that bout of pneumonia. She was so white, so innocent—with four strong men tromping over her body.

Meanwhile, backstage, the Snake Man waited night after night. The Snake Man was so withered and sallow, no one could guess his age. He might even have been a young man still.

He was the highlight of the whole institution, though he got the worst pay. He coiled himself into countless contortions, you'd think his heart would pop out from his body, he set the spectators' own vertebrae cracking—he was a Snake Man par excellence. With huge, green, good-natured eyes.

Every night after Anette's number with infinite care he'd drape around her shoulders the ermine cloak that was his very own. When she came home in the wee hours, he'd make her a hot tea. He dried her shoes at his tiny cast-iron stove.—Anna, he'd say (he never called her anything but Anna), one of these days you're going to go to the dogs.

And that time in Brno when the mayor's son proposed to her two days before his wedding and then stood her up when she waited for three hours in the rain behind the big carousel and came down with pneumonia—a thing she'd never do today, not even for Herr Willy—that time it was the Snake Man who filled in for her number, who fetched the doctor and had her taken to hospital. Then, being a man with a strong sense of duty, he hit the road with the rest of the troupe.

Oh, God, what a crazy life. Much too much and nothing that does you any good. That Marschall would throw fits if she knew what goes on in a circus caravan. But she doesn't anything about anything.

Confound it, there's been yet another impossible scene. Yet again involving Axel. Why am I so upset?

I—I'll write a letter of apology. I never should have gone—He didn't even really invite me. He was just being polite. Because he's a classy person. Didn't want to hurt my feelings. I don't belong in his company. And then that vulgar song! How he smirked. Axel! Everyone else can smirk, for all I care. But Axel—what on earth must he think of me? And that gesture he made as he helped me into my coat—

No, I shan't write Grete an apology. That silly goose! My song wasn't so awful that she had to run out of the room. But I'll write Axel. He mustn't think that I'm 'that kind of girl'. I never knew I love him. I worship him. He's a hundred, a thousand times handsomer than Doctor Alexander. I'll sneak into his lectures. He has a voice like the church organ when incense fills the air. I'll write him today. I'm sorry I sang that dirty song. I'm sorry—dear Jesus, there are so many things I'm sorry about. I could practically cry.

This morning at the library—

Oh, I'm never going to write about Herr Zaunegger again. Herr Zaunegger has no business here, that person's nothing but a fluke, a joke, a bad joke at that.

In fact, everything's a fluke. I could be rich, rich enough not to need anyone's presents. Or I could have grown up under milk-glass lamps, sheltered, loved, protected. All I need to do is ring and the maid brings me lemonade.

A fine gentleman, that Zaunegger! Those rows first thing in the morning. Today he even used the word whore. Meaning me. What do I care. But how can you even shake hands with someone like Axel when you and someone like Herr Zaunegger—

No, no, I shan't write any more about him. Anyway, do I always have to tell the truth? Is there a law about that? I could equally well write that Axel sits up nights just like Doctor Rüdiger, elbows propped on his desk, thinking of me, of me alone, he's promised to be faithful to Grete, six letters to me are hiding in the drawer, he groans, a tear drops on the blotting paper—but when he comes, when he suddenly comes at last, flinging open the door, Grete can drop dead, what does he care, he's coming, coming to me—

No, no, never! That's not the truth, mustn't ever be. Herr Zaunegger's the only truth, he's deep inside me, he's been with so many whores that—now I'm turning black about the mouth myself.

But Fräulein Marschall is going to be Frau Zaunegger and one day she'll get sick and won't understand what's wrong, won't know what that sickness is called—a stupid old maid like that knows nothing whatsoever.

Yesterday I went to see Ulla. I tried to sound her out a bit about symptoms and so on. But she wasn't even listening. The chief physician has the flu. Fever. He has a nurse of his own. Incidentally, Ulla thinks I'm hysterical. She's prescribing me bromides.

Axel's coming, he comes to see me nearly every day now. His household's in a state as if it were the lying-in again already, though the baby won't come for another three months. He's harried and unhoused. The moment he enters my room, the electric bulb flickers on, the air turns gold and everything's filled with reverence.

I go to his lectures. It's unfathomable that such an important intellect isn't world-famous yet. He simply must go to America. If only his domestic circumstances didn't squelch all his vital energies.

I'm convinced, I know it for sure, beyond a doubt, I feel the blackness about my mouth, a perpetual burning, and—it's hideous. If I end up in the hospital, the chief physician might bend over my bed. But Axel must never touch me again. He thinks I'm crazy, he's uncomprehending. I—I can't say it to his face. I won't let him through my door again. It's out of the question. Why aren't I Grete's chambermaid? Why can't I polish his shoes, organize his neckties, dust his desk? That's the only thing I want.

Ulla says I'm perfectly healthy. She doesn't understand at all. I'll go see the chief physician as soon as he's taking appointments again.

Axel isn't just unhoused. Axel is voracious. Oh God! I won't, I won't. All I want is to polish his shoes. Today he nearly struck me. I love him.

Now it's as hot as it was in a certain glaring loud spring, when all the girls wore filmy blouses, Doctor Alexander taught class in his shirtsleeves and not even the director could object. Often, I go on jaunts to the countryside, but the meadows are all too smooth and sleek, and confetti is scattered through the woods.

I want to fling myself into damp leaves and lush grass. I want permission to lie naked and kick until the smell of the earth creeps into all my pores. Maybe a monkey will hop onto my belly. Yellow flowers all around and a sky of heavy blue. Fullness, fullness and desire . . .

But instead, wearing my flowered dress—a pink circle drawn around each little bouquet, clearance sale, last one—I go back to the library morning after morning. The paint's melting on the shelves. The books stick. How much longer can all this go on.

I can't take it any more. The shop windows have turned into huge glass caves, the mirrors are sheets of water under rainy skies. Empty, everything's empty. The only stirring of life's on the movie screen. But yesterday the sad heroine who was cast out, scorned and insulted looked like the stranger again. I ran out in the middle. Which was foolish, because the plot was sure to turn out fine. A happy end is what they call it.

Anette's angry at me, by the way. She doesn't want to see me, always has some new excuse.

Something's the matter. She can't be afraid of me, can she. What is it this time! But something's the matter. Everything's the matter.

It can't turn out well.

I'll go away. Maybe a travelling circus will take me. Because Axel mustn't kiss me. He's the only one who must never know, not under any circumstances. Because I love him.

Yesterday he made a pass under a dark bush of rotting lilac. Courting couples all around on the benches. A blurry moon behind bars. I nearly screamed. A policeman noticed.

Axel silently escorted me home.—Go to your wife, I told him.

Why isn't that wife of his waiting up for him? Why doesn't she make him tea when he comes home, why doesn't she plump his cushions? Always self-absorbed, that wife is. Why doesn't she put another woman to bed with him, a good, beautiful, healthy woman? Why doesn't she help him, why—I'll go and see Ulla. Oh, Ulla's always thinking of her chief physician, someone like Axel's just a toy for her, or at best a pleasant narcotic.

Perhaps Anette—oh, I must be utterly mad.

Axel says so too. Well, he doesn't say 'mad', you don't use that kind of word in broad daylight without immediately calling the ambulance brigade. He says crazy. He thinks I'm crazy because I love him, because I don't care a bit whether, oh, fiddlesticks, I'd love him even if I had no mouth to kiss him with—

He doesn't understand that. Why should he. He's got his physics, his experiments. He's not here just to love some foolish female like me. He's here to become a great and famous man.

How dare she drag him down! That, that—

I'll strangle her.

This morning there wasn't just a row, there was a scandal. And now I'm the librarian with the steady pay, the health insurance and the pension fund no longer—what am I now, anyway?

But it was too too funny. I called him a swine, Zaunegger, that is. Seems no one had called him that before, and it was high time, too. I enjoyed it.

Marschall witnessed it, of course, and two elderly assistants and a student. A magnificent scene! Whatever was that man thinking? He's been hopping mad at me all these past weeks. And no wonder, I'm far too good for him.

—Now, missy, that simply won't do, he said when I got in twenty minutes late. His moustache bristled. There was something stuck to it, maybe a bit of milk skin from his breakfast coffee, and I couldn't help laughing and called him a swine.

That was some scandal! Marschall shrieked, both the assistants ran over to hold her, otherwise she might have swooned, that delicate betrothed, and Herr Zaunegger yelled, lobster-red and hoarse, arm outstretched:—Get you, you vulgar creature! Well, it's true, I hadn't exactly acted genteel.

Whatever will Axel say? Thinking of him, I don't feel quite right about it. He'll probably think I'm crazy again. He always does these days. I asked him to come visit this evening. God knows what tomorrow will bring.

Oh, right, I forgot to mention that my landlady is turning me out, cool as can be. Firstly, I owe rent and secondly the bailiff's been here three times already and the last time he pasted slips of paper on my things because I missed a couple of instalments on the fur. That's a pretty kettle of fish!

Everything's hopeless. And that's all for the best. Today Axel's coming, I bought him wonderful big heart cherries and a grapefruit, his favourite. Tomorrow I'll be gone, on a country road, in a station waiting room, in a train compartment or a circus caravan. Destination unknown.

Where on earth is Axel? I don't understand it, he's usually so punctual. It's already 9.15. From sheer boredom, I got my scribblings back out of the drawer. Do they count as impounded too? Axel should be here any moment, any moment. Nothing could have happened, could it. He's so awfully careless with his car. In the end it'll turn out he's dead. Axel—

Goodness me, it's not that terribly late. As long as 9.30 hasn't struck, there's really no call to get upset. It's pointless. Today the grapefruit's not as big as it usually is. I'll cut it open and sugar it for him.

Still not here. 9.45. Maybe I ought to call the police without further delay. Surely he wouldn't be angry at me. Oh God, these ghastly slips of paper from the bailiffs. My place really doesn't look very homely. I'll get some water and soak them all off. He's sure to come by the time I'm finished.

10.30. I've eaten three of the cherries.

11.30. I know where he is.

12.00. No, no, it mustn't be. It's Grete's fault. She made him do it. She was always so virtuous. At school she never noticed how Doctor Alexander needed to hear her voice. If you're like Grete, it's not right to want a man, a real live man. It's all the same to her what happens with him, if he goes to some girl on the street, as long as the kitchen's clean and gleaming and the cook is paid up and happy.

She doesn't even know what time he comes home.

But I, I, I'm waiting up for him. I can't help him, but I—

12.10. Grete must die.

In a certain circus, where the Snake Man contorted his heart out, and even owned an ermine cape, there was an old gypsy woman. A wild creature who could lay cards like no one else could. And she knew all kinds of little methods. Not poison, oh no, much, much sneakier.

You take a picture of your hated rival, a naked picture and a long darning needle heated in a flame, cross yourself three times and don't forget to bolt all your doors to ward off evil—

I don't have a picture of Grete, but I'd like to take a long darning needle and—

It wouldn't be decent of me not to add what happened afterward. Otherwise people might really think I was a murderess, a blasphemous, superstitious creature. Some would even claim I was to blame for Grete's death.

I mustn't let that happen. Now that more than ten months have passed, I consider it my duty to truthfully relate the extent to which I was and remain embroiled in all these incidents and twists of fate and how chance or providence chose to lead me back inside the bounds of everyday life.

And it would be ungrateful if I were to take all these wild, desperate, fantastical pages, this patchwork of different handwritings, and burn them in the stove. They lent me succour and support. As I wrote at the beginning: AND THE WORD BECAME FLESH.

That's why this book must go out into the world to those who are lonely and no match for their loneliness. We know so little about each other. Far too little. Or else it wouldn't be so very hard to be alone. Or else thousands of people wouldn't have to seek comfort and gratification in the joys and woes of someone like Brigitte Helmer. For we are pitiful and humble.

But I had the temerity to burst the bounds of fate. Even as a child I felt Horky's paper-stiff blouse against my chest, Grete's golden downy hair curled at my nape, Ulla's haughtiness shook me to the core, I played with Anette's tentacle fingers, I hated the stranger. Don't go thinking that I'm something special. We're all very much alike. And I never would have got to that point if Uncle Max hadn't vanished from my sight that salty North Sea afternoon. I was too deeply anchored in him to be sufficient unto myself after that. And so, I loved and lived with the others.

But now my days have turned simple and narrow. And that is a good thing. Because I am a simple, narrow person.

I'll try to tell it all in order.

Towards morning, after a night spent waiting for Axel in vain, I drank a half-full vial of opium that happened to be on my nightstand. Giddy and childish as I was at that time, I thought that would be enough to end my torments.

But I was awakened, someone shook me, calling my name over and over. I opened my eyes. The room was aswim in the red afternoon sun and Anette was standing by my side.

To see Anette, of all people, standing at my bedside gave me quite a turn. I sank into the cushions, feeling like an empty sack, a sensation that dogged me the whole time, incidentally, until—until the miracle occurred.

Anette was sobbing out loud, bawling really, and then, in fits and snatches, she told me that Grete had died that night. Of a miscarriage.

However appalling it seems to me now, I felt nothing, not a thing. When Anette asked me to come with her to the house where Grete lay dead—by herself she'd be afraid, but we had to go to Axel, Ulla was there expecting me—I got dressed mechanically and went along.

I can't remember how we got there, I don't know whether we went on foot, in a car or with the tram, all I know is that as we climbed the stairs, I felt I'd lived through it all before, so it wasn't really important. There was a smell of dead flowers, the clock in the living room had stopped, an open book lay on the mantlepiece.

The windows were curtained and amid her lace pillows Grete lay cold and stiff. Was that really Grete? She had a severe, pointy face like—

Today I'm ashamed to say it. But I wanted to tell things in order and true to the facts. Standing at the foot of Grete's bed, what I saw cold and stiff before me was the stranger.

My heart stood still.

Axel was crying and the maids were crying and Ulla and Anette were crying. They were all so stunned that they didn't notice the little boy crying in the nursery. But because nothing mattered at all to me and I felt like an empty sack—I have to repeat this to make it clear that I was relatively rational, though of course it's a higher form of rationality to follow a dead woman in death—I went to the little boy and soothed him. But he went on crying and I realized that he was wet, I got a fresh diaper from the blue baby dresser and put it on him. He calmed down and soon fell asleep.

I stayed by his side, and as he lay before me in his crib, I suddenly realized how he smelled of almond soap. I saw the baby's big gentle curving mouth, Grete's mouth, and it was as though someone I didn't know was reminding me how I'd broken my oath to the woman with the paralysed legs.

Ulla tried to usher me out of the house. She admitted later on that I'd seemed utterly devastated. As though I wasn't quite all there. She was probably right. I wasn't all there. And that was why she took me home.

It was night time already, and we couldn't open the door. The key was inside in the lock. We turned on the light and there were all my things in a pile outside the door. The landlady had thrown me out.

Ulla asked me a few quick questions, packed my belongings and all at once we were in Bea's house, at Mama's door.

I don't know how to describe what happened next. It was too miraculous, and though I'd made up my mind to write rationally—well—all at once the well-brushed smell of my childhood's velvet curtains wafted in my face, I woke up (I don't know how else to put it) and Uncle Max was lounging between those curtains.

He'd arrived from India that very day.

It doesn't matter what happened next, that Mama put me to bed and Bea asked excited questions, that Ulla attempted some hoarse explanation and *Herr von . . .* wanted to call a doctor. I suddenly felt an intense, purely physical pain at Grete's death, and heard Uncle Max pacing up and down next door, with long strides, Papa's strides, and once he said in his brown voice, Papa's voice, something like 'didn't look after her'.

Yes, they hadn't looked after me. And worst of all, I hadn't looked after myself. Uncle Max was the only one who'd understood that. After all, he also knew how you can love a shell, an ordinary shell in the sand.

What comes next is very simple. Uncle Max read this book (incidentally, he's for getting it published too, not under my name, of course) and he took me to the North Sea that summer.

It was glaring and glorious. And Uncle Max was most glorious of all. We wandered endless dunes in the splendour of the shell-shimmering afternoons. He was always a few steps ahead of me, his shoulders slightly bowed, his hands vaguely groping. And so he gropes his way around the whole world. Shortly after that he left for Greenland.

Papa was a banker. Bea married that *Herr von* . . . . Uncle Max has grown old. But he can't comprehend, and never will, that he's to have just one life as a human being. He loses himself to the sea and the sand, animals and stars. He'll vanish over and over again. And one day he won't ever come back.

I could have stayed with him. Or I could have died or gone back to being a librarian again at a different library with a different Herr Zaunegger. Incidentally, I wrote the real Herr Zaunegger an apology. I could have gone off to America to be a nurse or I could have lived with Bea and helped raise her children, my family's awfully kind to me really, and I could have travelled to Paris with Anette. Though I don't know if she's there alone. Or I could have asked Ulla to help find me a job or a man, she's a brilliant doctor, by the way, it was true that I hadn't got sick from Herr Zaunegger, I could have—

There are hundreds of things I could have done. But in mirrors and shop windows all I ever saw was one figure. Familiar to me, intimately known. Pale and resolute. The stranger. Me. The only one.

Then Axel came and asked me to stay. For a moment I thought of Uncle Max, but I had a horror of the endless backdrop blurring behind him. Axel has good, strong arms. He's kind to me and he trusts me. The boy has his figure, though he has Grete's mouth and her gentle moist eyes. A child with those eyes needs cherishing.

I'm going to marry Axel. A real proper marriage with a bedroom, kitchen and phone. Ulla would never do that. She'd consider it sacrilegious towards the dead. But life is small, and what more you can do than be good to each other. Why should Axel go searching for someone else, unhoused and hungry again? Anette's not right for him. And I'm not Anette. I don't feel any sense of guilt.

It's best this way for me and for him. I'll be a good wife. There'll be little vexations and little joys, for the daily life of the individual is neither grand nor miraculous. I'll think of Grete when he goes off in search of other women. I'll mourn for her in silence.

But if one day my child, my daughter—perhaps she'll resemble the stranger, perhaps she'll console me for the lonely light of the shaded evening lamps—if she should stand enkindled and entranced beside a sunburned man, I'll vanish into the next room, quietly, all alone. I'll know to stay within my bounds.—

• • • •

EDITOR'S ACKNOWLEDGEMENTS

I thank Kathleen Dunmore, Maria Lazar's granddaughter, for her warm hospitality in Nottingham, her energetic commitment to her grandmother's legacy and the trust that from the very outset she placed in me as her publisher and editor; Johann Sonnleitner for his valuable work as the editor of Maria Lazar's first three novels; Veronika Zwerger, director of the Austrian Exile Library at the Vienna Literature House, for facilitating our study of Lazar's posthumous papers; Maria Teuchmann and the team at Sessler Verlag for their ongoing efforts to bring Lazar's plays to the stage; Isabel Fargo Cole for the magnificent English translation; and last but not least Oliver Lubrich, my thesis advisor at the University of Bern, whose constant advice and encouragement keeps alive my enthusiasm for the consciousness-expanding force of literature and my delight in literary scholarship.

Albert C. Eibl

Translated by Isabel Fargo Cole

WE ARE HER UNKNOWN READERS

AN HOMAGE TO THE INDOMITABLE MARIA LAZAR (1895–1948)

Afterword to the Original German Edition by Albert C. Eibl

Translated by Isabel Fargo Cole

I

In September 2022, in my capacity as publisher, I was invited to Nottingham by Maria Lazar's granddaughter Kathleen Dunmore. Following her mother Judith's death at an advanced age in early 2020, she was finally taking possession of the posthumous papers that her enigmatic grandmother had meticulously organized shortly before committing suicide in Stockholm in 1948. Until now, the papers had slumbered for over six decades in two black metal boxes hidden under a coverlet in the Dunmore family's Northampton living room. For Judith Dunmore, Maria Lazar's papers had been a non-negotiable taboo. The memory of her mother's protracted illness and suicide—

she electrocuted herself with a hairdryer in the bathtub—was simply too painful. As, no doubt, was the memory of her two unmarried aunts who were murdered by the Waffen-SS in the Belarusian death camp Maly Trostinec in late August 1942. Not once were Judith's children allowed to open the boxes.

Now, at last, the moment had come. The granddaughter was ready to break the spell. Having been denied the chance to meet her talented grandmother while she was still alive, she wanted at least to get to know her through her unpublished works. On behalf of the Austrian Broadcasting Corporation, the screenwriter and director Kerstin Schütze accompanied me to Nottingham, documenting the journey in search of Maria Lazar and the process of sifting through her papers. Together with Kathleen, we opened the boxes to reveal a treasure trove. The unpublished novels and novellas included *Zwei Soldaten* (Two Soldiers), *Der Walzer im Hof* (The Waltz in the Courtyard), *Det kam af sig selv* (As Though of Its Own Accord)—a novel commemorating the courageous Danish resistance against the Nazi occupation—and, last but not least, *Viermal ICH* (Myself, Four Times). And in addition to a handful of completed but never-performed plays such as *Der blinde Passagier* (The Stowaway), *Die Hölle auf Erden* (Hell on Earth), *Die Weiber von Lynö* (The Women of Lynö) and *Die Liebe höret niemals auf* (Love Never Faileth), there were more than 35 short stories and political essays, numerous articles, two ideas for films, a radio play and ten poems.

In 2023, this literary gold mine was donated to the Austrian Exile Library at the Vienna Literature House, where it is now being studied and edited for publication in the city where Maria Lazar came of age as a writer and which, at least until 1933, she regarded as her intellectual home.

II

Who was Maria Lazar? Born in 1895 as the youngest child of a well-off assimilated Jewish family—her father was a high-ranking Austrian railway official—she attended the famous Schwarzwald school on Franziskanerplatz in Vienna's First District. Run by the prominent salonnière Eugenie Schwarzwald on the principles of the New Education movement, it was considered one of Europe's most progressive schools for girls. Some classes were even taught by major intellectuals like Adolf Loos, Arnold Schönberg and Oskar Kokoschka—who in 1916 immortalised the young Lazar in his painting *Lady with a Parrot*. At Schwarzwald's salon in the Josefstadt district, the precocious and highly gifted young writer rubbed shoulders with other prominent cultural figures such as Jakob Wassermann, Egon Friedell, Robert Musil, Peter Altenberg and Hermann Broch. Lazar went on to study history and philosophy at the University of Vienna, while occasionally teaching classes at the Schwarzwald schools in Vienna's First District and the town of Semmering. 1920 saw her literary debut with the expressionist roman à clef *Die Vergiftung* (The Poisoning). In 1921 her one-act play *Der Henker* (The Executioner), published by the Drei Masken Verlag in Munich, had its premiere, given a lengthy if mixed review by the famous critic Alfred Polgar in the *Weltbühne*.

In 1922, she launched her journalistic career at the prestigious Viennese daily *Der Tag*, which counted Alfred Polgar, Robert Musil, Béla Balázs and Joseph Roth among its regular contributors. By 1933, Lazar had published more than 100 essays, political commentaries and reviews in the resolutely liberal left-wing newspaper, soon gaining a reputation as an acerbic and perspicacious journalist. In 1923, Lazar married fellow journalist Friedrich Strindberg, son of the playwright Frank Wedekind and Frieda Uhl, who was married to the Swedish playwright August Strindberg at the time of his birth. Though the marriage did not last, it allowed Lazar to acquire Swedish citizenship. When she fled to Sweden in 1939 to escape the advancing German army, this protected her from deportation; otherwise, as a Jew, she probably would not have survived World War II.

Maria Lazar and her young daughter Judith had already gone into exile in Denmark in 1933, joining her childhood friend, the actress Helene Weigel, and Weigel's husband Bertolt Brecht at the home of the Danish writer Karin Michaelis on the island of Thurø. There, she translated numerous English, Danish and Swedish novels into German for prominent publishers such as S. Fischer and Kiepenheuer.(For instance, in 1928 Maria Lazar produced the first German translation of F. Scott Fitzgerald's *The Great Gatsby*, reissued by Kampa in 2025 to mark the epochal novel's 100th anniversary.) From then on, she was forced to write much of her work 'for the drawer'. Not for lack of effort, she was no longer able to publish her challenging, multifaceted novels in Austria, Germany or Switzerland. For one thing, they had a political dimension, an openly oppositional and subversive message. For another, back as far as 1930, the Nazi's anti-Semitic cultural ideology had unofficially infiltrated and influenced the entire German-speaking region, and after the Nazis seized power in 1933, repressive laws prevented Jews from publishing in Germany.

In Denmark, she wrote works such as *Die Eingeborenen von Maria Blut* (The Natives of Maria Blut), while keeping part of Walter Benjamin's Berlin library safe from the Nazis. With the outbreak of World War II, even Denmark was no longer safe, so Lazar emigrated with her daughter to Stockholm, where she played a key role in the exile scene during the years to come. After a long, untreatable illness

(Morbus Cushing), embittered and disappointed at the lack of recognition for her literary work, she took her own life in 1948.

III

Like many other Austrian women writers disowned and persecuted in the Third Reich—such as Hermynia zur Mühlen, Anna Gmeyner, Else Feldmann, Mela Hartwig, Grete Hartwig-Manschinger and Marta Karlweis—until just a few years ago Maria Lazar had been utterly forgotten. Her name was nowhere to be found in the pertinent literary histories and encyclopaedias. Internet searches turned up next to nothing. And while her sister Auguste Lazar had managed to bring about the posthumous publication of *The Natives of Maria Blut*—her prescient novel about Nazism's emergence in rural Austria—in 1958 in East Germany, no other editions of her works were available.

Even in the case of *The Poisoning*, the Austrian National Library had just one single copy available—and it was missing its cover. When I first read this pugnacious debut by a gifted malcontent, I was profoundly impressed. Never before had upper-class Vienna's moral hypocrisy in the waning years of the Habsburg Empire been skewered in language so relentlessly scathing. Even the great Karl Kraus' withering critique of society and its class structure seemed almost conciliatory by contrast. For all the malice of his trenchant reviews and rants, Kraus ultimately remains far too entangled in the finely knit web of convention to deal the conservative bourgeoisie a genuine death blow. But the young Lazar brims with glee, giving powerful voice to a manic urge to shatter the world to smithereens as she tramples the still-warm corpses of her victims, the wishy-washy and the bigoted whom she would later identify as precursors of the

Fascist movement's willing accessories: 'Today the light blindingly pierced stones and her body's rigid skin. It dripped from the leaves, hot and glaring, redolent of the blood of all the people walking down the street. The blue was too deep, woven from rebellious forces.' These words appeared in 1920's *The Poisoning*, whose alleged 'obtrusively female smell' had Thomas Mann tut-tutting in his maudlin diaries upon its publication, whereas Robert Musil noted the young writer's 'ruthlessly objective gaze' and 'nimble and forceful characterizations'. He expected great things from her talent, and he was certainly right about that. Maria Lazar's epic and dramatic work to come would be woven from rebellious poetic forces, never hesitating to call barbarism by its right name in all its different guises, or to demand moral righteousness. She left a legacy of uncompromising artistic fortitude in the face of modern urban life's deromanticized barrenness and the banality of a barren age's evil.

IV

The reissue of Lazar's feisty debut *The Poisoning* and *The Natives of Maria Blut* in late 2014 by my newly founded Viennese publishing house *Das vergessene Buch* (The Forgotten Book)—dedicated from the outset to rescuing unjustly forgotten early-twentieth-century women writers from oblivion—launched the eventful rediscovery of the remarkable writer, journalist, dramatist and translator.

In December 2019, at Vienna's Akademietheater, Lazar's one-act play *The Executioner* premiered for the first time in nearly a century, ushering in the rediscovery of her hitherto forgotten work as a playwright. Another highlight of the author's gradual canonization was the staging of *The Natives of Maria Blut* by the ensemble of Vienna's

Burgtheater. Adapted for the stage by Alexander Kerlin and directed by Lucia Bihler, the play was lauded as one of the most remarkable productions on the German-language stage and featured at the Berliner Theatertreffen festival in January 2023. In 1935, in Danish exile, Lazar had already foreseen the terrible upheavals that would soon seize Europe and the world and located their epicentre not in the big city but in the Catholic countryside. Tectonic shifts begin in the factories, the marketplace, in afternoon coffee parties, at the hair salon, inevitably culminating in the breakdown of civilization when the archetype of the bitter little man claims the right to dominate the world stage.

Der Nebel von Dybern (The Fog of Dybern), a play about a disaster at a Belgian poison gas factory, had been staged in Stettin, Copenhagen and London starting in 1933, but sank into obscurity after 1935 and ceased to be performed. That changed in the fall of 2023, when the Theater Nestroyhof Hamakom in Vienna revived the highly topical anti-militarist drama. In February 2024 it was performed at the Schauspielhaus Graz, where it was followed by Lazar's satirical World War drama *Die Hölle auf Erden* (Hell on Earth), which had had its world premiere in the fall of 2024 at the Landestheater in Tyrol. In mankind's last days, God has gone into retirement and sends Saint Peter and two rascally angels to earth to save whatever can be saved. In the end, however, it's the Devil who staves off the next World War and awarded the Nobel Peace Prize.

In June 2025, at the Schauspielhaus Düsseldorf, this was followed by the world premiere of what is probably Lazar's most mature and dramaturgically ambitious play, *The Stowaway*: A German Jew on the run from the Gestapo hides in the cargo hold of a Danish packet vessel. When he is discovered by the crew, it sets off a debate about obedience and betrayal, moral courage, responsibility and the inevitability of callousness in the face of catastrophe.

In early 2020, thanks to Lazar's grandnephew Markus Oezelt, I was the first to read the original German typescript of Lazar's Depression-era thriller *Leben verboten!* (No Right to Live!), long believed to be lost. Shortly thereafter, during the pandemic, summer 2020, I was able to publish it to a huge media response. As a strongly anti-fascist novel with a subversive, oppositional subtext, for obvious reasons the work could initially be published only in an abridged English edition in London in 1934. In what may be her most suspenseful novel, written in Vienna between 1930 and 1932, Lazar's breath-taking use of cinematic editing techniques evokes the shimmering, nightmarish unreality of the years preceding the Nazis' seizure of power in Germany. The millstones of a menacing new era threaten to crush a man without qualities, the Jewish banker Ernst von Ufermann, who assumes a new identity following a plane crash and ends up smuggling a mysterious package from Berlin to Vienna for a gang of young Nazi revolutionaries. Here Lazar shows how easily a passive individual can unwittingly become the plaything of forces whose destructive potential may be realized too late.

V

Myself, Four Times, Lazar's second novel, was written in the late 1920s when she was still living in Vienna. It, too, went unpublished in the wake of the stock market crash and the rise of the swastika—despite the fact that it barely touches on politics. In 1929, she offered the manuscript to several Swiss publishers as well as Zsolnay-Verlag in Vienna, but without success. Jewish authors were already facing an increasingly oppressive atmosphere in German-speaking countries. And so, she resorted to a subterfuge for her next novel *Veritas verhext die Stadt* (Veritas Puts a Hex on the City). She wrote the book under the Scandinavian-sounding pseudonym Esther Grenen and posed as the translator of what she claimed was an unknown but promising new Danish writer. The daring sleight-of-hand paid off: the publishing house Kiepenheuer Verlag fell for it and serialized the novel in the *Berliner Tageblatt* in early 1930 and in the popular Viennese magazine *Der Kuckuck* from November 1931. It was a great popular success. From then on, the writer Maria Lazar ceased to be, while the author Esther Grenen began to lead a highly productive life of her own. *Myself, Four Times* would be the last novel that Lazar wrote under her own name.

This picaresque, simultaneously cheeky, disturbing and entertaining, tells of the friendship between four very different girls in the precarious years of crisis before and after the end of World War I. Together, they go to school, come of age and go through a series of emotional upheavals that—almost against their will—strengthen their idiosyncratic, schizophrenic group identity. The nameless narrator records the girls' daily life, their erotic adventures and entanglements, their yearnings and their pretensions in a 'confession' that increasingly takes on a manic quality. The identity of the city where the main action plays out is deliberately left open. Vienna is never mentioned. The novel could equally well be set in Berlin, Hamburg, Munich or any other large German-speaking city where the lost World War has brought economic hardship and loss of status to large swathes of the population, who suffer from a tenacious sense of existential anxiety and 'transcendental homelessness' (Georg Lukàcs). Love is repeatedly exposed as an illusion, economic survival is constantly jeopardized and even family bonds are unable to offer ultimate security; casual amusement, irresponsible shenanigans and the opportunistic exploitation of one's own body as a standard means of payment and social advancement offer the only escape from an everyday life deromanticized by industrialization and mass culture. Or, at least, they are better than nothing.

In a narrative strategy resembling Irmgard Keun's in *Gilgi, eine von uns* (Gilgi, One of Us, 1931) or in her 'women's novel' *Das kunstseidene Mädchen* (The Artificial Silk Girl, 1932), *Myself, Four Times* presupposes the kind of fundamental disillusionment typical of the literature of the New Objectivity.

The protagonists are Grete, the beautiful, unapproachable professor's daughter; the cheeky, provocative and sensuous Anette; the unattractive but keenly intelligent Ulla and the hypersensitive narrator. For all four of them, life as a woman in the male-dominated, appearance-fixated, posing, not-so-golden Twenties presents itself as a succession of bitter disappointments, unexpected calamities and psychologically overwhelming acts of violence. In a chatty, flippant, hyper-animated tone—with numerous flashbacks, unexpected cuts and cinematic sequences—this experience is distilled into an impressionistic microcosm of emotion and language whose stylistic sophistication far surpasses Irmgard Keun and other contemporary authors, masterfully anticipating prismatic aesthetic techniques and narrative fragmentation found in the postmodern novel.

But what is the meaning of the mirage-like leitmotif of the 'stranger' who appears to the narrator in mirrors, display windows or other reflective surfaces whenever—so it seems—traumatic events need to be suppressed?

'The stranger' stands—not solely, but surely in part—for the Freudian 'Id': the unconscious that ultimately cannot be suppressed and inevitably forces its way to the surface of the personality, with catastrophic consequences for the ego. *Myself, Four Times* is about these consequences, about the perils of what goes unlived and suppressed, and last but not least about the therapeutic power of writing: 'When mirrors fail, shop windows and the glass balls, cut-glass inkwells and polished tabletops, maybe then words will help, the written word. As the saying goes: AND THE WORD BECAME FLESH . . . . . .'

Vienna
January 2026

TRANSLATOR'S NOTE

Lazar's idiosyncratic, expressionistic style is a pleasure and a challenge to translate. Of special note in *Myself, Four Times* is the way certain images, words or phrases associated with certain characters or situations are repeated throughout the novel. I have done my best to retain these crucial leitmotifs, which structure the work and reflect the narrator's obsessive mental state.

Isabel Fargo Cole